Searching for the Shire

*One Woman's Quest
For Independence*

Florence St. John

Maison

Vero Beach, Florida
The Hibiscus City
lamaisonpublishing@gmail.com

Happiness is like a butterfly
The more you chase it,
The more it eludes you.
But if you turn your attention
to other things,
It will come and sit softly
on your shoulder...

David Thoreau

Author's Note

Codependency! I used to roll my eyes when I heard the word. Then, one day, I stumbled across a YouTube video by life coach and codependency expert Lisa Romano. She described the very feelings and turmoil I'd carried throughout my life. It was surreal—someone finally understood my pain and confirmed what I'd been feeling all along.

Lisa said that the roots of codependency often begin with emotional abandonment or abuse in childhood. I never thought of myself as abused, but her words stayed with me. I grew up in a dysfunctional family. My father was an alcoholic, though no one acknowledged it. He sat at the kitchen table, drinking Burgundy wine from a gallon jug, brooding over his life. The smallest noise, even the sound of a closing cabinet or a spoon dropping to the floor, could set off his rage. My mother escaped to bingo almost every night, leaving my siblings and me to deal with him. It made me anxious, but I learned to put my mother's needs before mine while sidestepping my father's retaliation.

"You have an emotional splinter," Lisa said, "but with the right tools, you could remove it and heal."

She explained that boundaries weren't ultimatums, but values we honor and defend. That was my problem. My values had always been weak and easily compromised. Avoiding conflict was everything to me.

My greatest fear was that if I made the wrong move, the people I loved might get angry and leave. The thought was so unbearable that I couldn't even let myself imagine it.

For the first time, my life began to make sense. I had learned to repress my emotions, to avoid confrontation with my father, and to please my mother in exchange for her love.

"It's not your fault," Lisa said. "It's your programming. You've been brainwashed to suppress your emotions."

My codependency was a by-product of unprocessed childhood trauma. I wasn't inadequate or unlovable, just damaged. Maybe that's why I never felt good enough.

Lisa Romano shed light on that dark place where I stored my pain. A place even I couldn't reach. I still had questions, but I knew where to find the answers. They were waiting in my childhood, and I would have to go back to find them.

Chapter 1 | Women's Movement

1968

My mother tuned in to the small black-and-white television in the living room to watch the women's liberation movement take shape. A group of female activists protested outside the Atlantic City Convention Center during the Miss America Pageant. The women surrounded a *Freedom Can*, in which they threw their bras, high-heeled shoes, and curlers, deeming them *instruments of female torture*. While some women railed against those who held traditional roles, my mother seemed content to be a stay-at-home mom.

Every morning, she'd hustle my siblings and me out of the house and out of her hair. While we were at school, she had the whole day to herself: a little cleaning, a little shopping, and a few soap operas. I envied her life and wished I could stay home, too. She wasn't particularly happy, but she didn't have to deal with the hurts and stresses of society. In my eyes, my mother had freedom. Freedom at home.

"Florence!" She called from the bottom of the stairs. "You're going to be late for school!"

Remembering I hadn't done my social studies homework, I buried my head in the pillow. It was my first year of junior high school, and I was supposed to write about what I wanted to be when I graduated from High School. After staring at a blank sheet of paper the night before, I had set it aside and reached for my book, *The Hobbit*, by J.R.R. Tolkien. Normally, I didn't read unless forced to at school, but I was captivated from the start. Hobbits lived in the Shire, an idyllic fictional place untouched by the pressures of the world. Although they were curious about adventures, they were homebodies and loved the simple life. The idea of this fantasy land was the perfect escape from my reality.

I tugged on my bell-bottomed jeans and sniffed a T-shirt to make sure it was clean, since my mother wasn't always up on laundry duties. I stared at myself in the bathroom mirror and frowned. I resembled my mother — Mediterranean complexion, brown hair, dark eyes, and a heart-shaped face.

My mother had convinced me to get a haircut the day before. She called it a pageboy. I thought I looked like the little boy on the paint can.

I could hear my parents arguing in the kitchen. It was a daily occurrence. From the time I could tie my shoes, I tried to stay out of the line of fire, but now, there was no avoiding them. Reluctantly, I went downstairs.

My father pushed past me to leave for work as if I were invisible. He was a handsome man... Dean Martin's looks and the same propensity for alcohol.

Sometimes, on the weekend, Dad would take my brother, sister, and me out so Mom could have the house to herself to clean. We'd go to the park or spend a few hours at the zoo. He was usually in a good mood, easygoing, and even fun, but we knew to tread carefully. One wrong word could flip the switch, and suddenly, the whole outing would feel different.

My mother was quite beautiful. She had a heart-shaped face and reddish-brown hair, which she swept up in a bun. She attracted the attention of other men wherever she went. This drove my father crazy.

She looked at me and tilted her head. "Your hair looks cute."

"I look like a boy!"

"Well, it's going to be much easier to take care of now that it's short." She handed me a buttered poppyseed roll. I took one bite and stopped.

"Where's my book bag?" I asked, forgetting about the roll. My mother had a habit of moving things or throwing them away when she was in cleaning mode. Fear washed over me at the thought of going to school without my books.

"It's in the hall closet," she said, "and don't forget to take a jacket. It's chilly today."

Relieved to find my bag, I obediently put on my jacket and ran out the front door.

"You should eat something," my mother called after me.

I went back and took the roll she had buttered for me, but once outside, I threw it in the bushes. Even though I was hungry, some of the boys at school pointed out that I had gained weight, and I felt fat.

As I navigated the path to school, I studied the cracks in the sidewalk and pulled my jacket tighter to my chest to hide my budding breasts. At thirteen, I developed before the other girls in my grade.

My pulse quickened with every step as I entered the classroom and quickly took my seat.

When I lived in Brooklyn, I was an above-average student. Then, my parents moved to Long Island.

Although the Brooklyn curriculum was one grade behind, the school gave me the benefit of the doubt and placed me in a Regents-level class, a prerequisite for college admission.

Math was my worst subject. The teacher, Mrs. Beck, was a steel-haired German woman. Her glasses perched on the edge of her nose as she surveyed the class. There was tension in the air. I closed my eyes and prayed. *Please don't call on me.* But it was no use.

"Florence, come up to the blackboard and show us the reduced form of this fraction."

My stomach did somersaults. Gulping hard, I made my way to the front of the classroom.

Mrs. Beck handed me a piece of chalk. I could feel her unwavering gaze as I raised it to the board.

She tapped her foot impatiently. "You need to find the common denominator first."

I took a deep breath and attempted to find the solution, but the method always eluded me. Was I supposed to divide or multiply?

Mrs. Beck's eyes narrowed. "You're putting the cart before the horse!"

The sound of my classmates snickering behind me made me freeze. All I could see was her judgmental face.

"Maybe if you had paid attention when I went over this in class, you'd understand, Florence! Go back to your seat."

Given permission to flee, I hurried back to my desk.

The last class of the day was social studies. Without the previous night's homework, I entered the classroom.

Ms. Barton was writing out a list of occupations on the blackboard. She was one of the youngest teachers in the school and an advocate who pushed against the stay-at-home mom fantasy. She told us that choosing to stay out of the workforce hurts gender equality.

"None of us lives on an island," she reminded us. "Choices matter!"

An island sounded good to me.

"Let's see what interesting jobs you've come up with," she said.

One by one, the students in the class stood up and boasted about their future careers. Boys wanted to be doctors or pilots. Girls wanted to be nurses or airline stewardesses. When my turn came, I moved my lips, but no sound emerged.

"Florence? What do you want to be?" Ms. Barton asked.

The class waited for my answer.

"A Hobbit," I muttered under my breath.

"Florence, please speak louder so we can hear you."

"She said a Hobbit!" the boy next to me yelled.

The class broke out in laughter.

Ms. Barton smacked her ruler on the desk to restore order in the classroom.

I wanted to crawl into a Hobbit hole and die. Luckily, the bell rang. I rushed out of the classroom.

On my way home, I took a shortcut through the woods, avoiding the bridge where class bullies often waited for the meek. I climbed over the fence that separated me from the whoosh of cars along the parkway. The stillness of the woods muffled my peers' condescending voices, and a comforting peace enveloped me.

Except for the squirrels, who protested furiously at my intrusion, the only sounds came from songbirds chirping above the trees and the occasional snapping of twigs under my feet. The sun angled through the trees in thin beams, and the rich smell of soil and moss drifted to my nose. I imagined traveling with the Hobbit's characters through forests and mythical places.

As I walked along a small stream, a screeching cry rose beyond the trees. It grew louder as I walked along the path. A sweet, murky smell of earth floated in the breeze. The stream widened and opened to a lake. The squawks were coming from a flock of birds. Osprey swooped over the water, feeding on fish and bugs near the surface as tiny frogs leaped around the water's edge. Tadpoles in various stages of growth swam around the shallows.

I followed a curved and twisted path until I came to a fork. Something urged me to go left, but the sun was setting through the trees, and it was getting late.

Once again, I found myself wondering what came next—what I truly wanted to do after high school. A career sounded exciting in theory, full of possibilities and newness. But beneath the surface shimmered a familiar fear: the expectation to be perfect. What if I wasn't smart enough? What if I tried and failed?

I turned down the right-hand path, the one that edged the woods and brushed up against backyards I knew by heart. At the end, where I usually climbed the chain-link fence, I stopped. Someone had cut the links—a ragged opening now gaped where there hadn't been one before. The barrier was gone, but I hesitated.

I'd always be a Hobbit at heart—longing for adventure, yet deeply rooted in the comfort of home.

Chapter 2 | Music

The yellow plastic adapter on my mother's 45 rpm record spun to life, and *Blame It on the Bosa Nova* filled the room. My mother danced around, singing along with the music. Steve Lawrence and Eydie Gorme were her favorites. Her favorite was *Go Away Little Girl.* Somehow, I thought they were singing it to me.

When she was a teenager, a Broadway agent heard her singing at a high school dance. He gave her his card and told her to visit him when she turned eighteen. But she met my father instead, and he put the kibosh on her career. Still, she managed to record two 78 rpm records in the city. I loved to play with them when my father wasn't around. When he was home, I begged my mother to play *Candy Girl* by the Four Seasons. It was such a happy song.

My older cousins, Beatrice and Flo, would take me along with them to the local pizza joint. They would set me up on a stool with a slice and then pump money into a jute box.

My Guy by Mary Wells filled my ears while I ate the best pizza and watched my cousins dance.

I was almost ten when the Beatles appeared on the Ed Sullivan Show. We watched it in the living room on our black-and-white television.

The British Invasion had begun. My cousin Gina used to watch a television show called *Where the Action Is*. It was a spin-off of Dick Clark's *American Bandstand*. Herman's Hermits sang *Mrs. Brown, You Have a Lovely Daughter*, and Paul Revere & the Raiders sang *Kicks*. I thought my cousin was so cool. A year older than me, she let me come with her to the roof when she wanted a smoke. She even let me try it.

A year later, Sonny and Cher came onto the scene. My cousin Jasonine used to sing along with the records. She made me sing Sonny's parts whenever I came to visit. I wouldn't say I liked that, but I understood. Jasonine's long brown hair draped down to her waist, and she fit Cher's part better.

At home, I had a small transistor radio. Sharing a room with my sister, Julia, I had little privacy. Sometimes, I piled my blankets under the hanging clothes in my bedroom closet to get away from her. I listened to Rolling Stone's *Goodbye Ruby Tuesday*. In the privacy of my closet, I let my tears flow.

Suddenly, the door of my closet swung open.

"What are you doing?" Julia asked.

"Nothing," I mumbled, scrambling out of my hiding place. After that, I listened to my music in the basement, sitting on the clothes dryer.

High school promised to be more exciting. It was my Sophomore year, and I had to find my way to each class on my own. Lost in a sea of students from other junior high schools. I clutched the map the counselor had given me and navigated through the crowded hallways. It was scary at first, but I eventually fell into a routine.

Elvis Presley was back from the Army, giving the Beatles a run for their money. My cousin Lee had plastered his posters all over her bedroom walls, but I wasn't interested. My music education continued in a different direction.

I had a male cousin who was a few years older than me. John had long, wavy hair and a full beard. He worked at Madison Square Garden and sometimes had access to free tickets. After getting my parents' permission, I accepted his invitation to see the Rolling Stones.

I was buzzing with excitement when John drove all the way to Long Island to pick me up. Even though he was family, driving to the city felt a little awkward.

When we arrived at Madison Square Garden, we had to pass a group of Hells Angels to get inside. We entered the auditorium through a haze of smoke. I was familiar with the smell of cigarette smoke, but something else mingled in the air. It was my first experience with marijuana. As joints were passed around, I hesitantly drew in the smoke and then passed it down to the person sitting next to me.

The lights went down, and the stage came alive. The opening act was Ike & Tina Turner.

Mick Jagger came out, and everyone jumped to their feet and cheered. He flipped around the stage in a red scarf, singing *Jumpin' Jack Flash*. I was mesmerized.

That summer, I spent months at concerts by Jimi Hendrix, Janis Joplin, and Cream, but they were a blur because I had become accustomed to smoking pot.

There was a big concert somewhere upstate. They called it Woodstock. I was only fifteen and too young to go. Women performers were coming into their own, with Grace Slick, Janis Joplin, and Joan Baez taking center stage. But I grew to love groups like The Who and Santana.

Once school started in the fall, I couldn't attend any more concerts. My freshman year in high school was marked by a heavy class schedule. Some students left the school in the afternoon to go to BOCES, a technical school, to learn a trade. I wondered why I hadn't been chosen to go.

Students were transported from other districts to diversify the racial landscape. They called it *busing*. No one was happy about it, especially the handful of Black students who found themselves surrounded by white kids.

Tensions rose, and riots broke out. After tables flew across the cafeteria, the school hired police officers to patrol the halls and stand guard at each building wing. Graffiti covered the walls.

Usually, after school, I spent hours in my room listening to The Doors on the stereo my father gave me for Christmas. He always made fun of the group's name.

"Why didn't they call themselves 'The Windows?' he'd ask and laugh at his own punchline.

I had a couple of good friends who shared my love of music. My best friend, Stacy, had very strict parents, so I often stayed over at her place. We'd stay up all night listening to Jethro Tull and playing crazy eights.

When we heard that Ten Years After was playing at the Fillmore East, we concocted a plan to get her out of her house. She snuck out of her window on the night of the concert, and we took the LIRR to the city. We had to walk several blocks to get to the concert hall, careful not to step on the sleeping bums in the street. Coming home in the middle of the night was risky, but we made it back alive.

Chapter 3 | Summer of Love

It was a warm, balmy evening on Long Island. I turned up my stereo to drown out my parents' arguing downstairs. Their fights were usually about money, sex, or the lack thereof. When everything fell silent, I went to the kitchen to find my mother alone.

"Florence, do you mind if I go to bingo at the church tonight?" she asked, but it wasn't really a question.

"Of course not," I replied.

"Great! Dinner is on the stove. I just need to get out. You understand, don't you?"

"Yes, Mom. Don't worry about me. I'll be fine."

There was always the risk that her absence would make my father angry, and he'd start drinking, so I made myself scarce and walked to the corner deli, hoping to see Bobby. He was an older boy who hung out in front of the stores. Two years my senior, his streetwise toughness left me in awe. He had long, straggly hair, but soulful eyes, and wore tight-fitting bell-bottoms.

Sure enough, he was there hanging out with his friends. I didn't think he even knew I was alive, so it took me by surprise when he looked my way.

"I like your pants," he said.

My heart raced. "Thanks. I made them myself."

"Do you want to go for a walk?" he said, linking his arm through mine.

I nodded, and we strolled down a dead-end street and sat on the curb at the edge of the woods. It was dark and secluded, the place where couples came to make out.

Bobby put his arm around my shoulder and pulled me closer. The smell of alcohol and cigarettes mingled on his breath as his lips touched mine.

At first, I was enjoying the moment. But soon, his hands crept up the back of my shirt, fumbling to unhook my bra.

"Stop," I said, pulling my shirt down. I could almost hear my mother's voice. — Be a good girl.

I let him kiss me again, but his hands kept crawling. I had to keep pulling my shirt down. After a few more attempts, he stood up.

"You're uptight and hung up. I have to go."

Uptight? Hung up?

I sat there feeling abandoned, watching him get farther and farther away.

Images of hippie chicks at Woodstock wearing only flowers around their necks flashed through my mind--Free Love and sexual liberation.

Most of my girlfriends had steady boyfriends, but not me. I was the only girl without one. Boys often asked me out on dates, but there was rarely a second date if they didn't get what they wanted.

Perhaps, maybe, I was just like my mother.

The next time I ran into Bobby, he nudged me playfully. "My parents are going out of town next week. Why don't you come over? I just scored some really good pot. We can listen to music and get high."

I wanted Bobby to be my boyfriend, so I decided right then and there. I would offer him my virginity.

On Monday, I skipped school and left my house, heading to Bobby's apartment. Scared about what I was about to do, I knocked. When Bobby opened his door, he wasn't wearing a shirt, which startled me. I tried not to look at his hairy chest and broad shoulders.

"I'm glad you decided to come over," he said, leading me to his room. We started making out immediately. His hand crept up my back. Instinctively, I pushed it away when he tried to unclasp my bra. I told myself to relax, and Bobby's kisses heated to a fevered pitch. Like a speeding train going down a track, there was no stopping once it started. Reality melted away as he peeled off my clothes. All I knew about sex was what I'd seen in the movies. Expecting something wonderful and romantic, I closed my eyes, anticipating an earthquake or at least a tremor, but all I felt was stabbing pain—then it was over, ending my status as a virgin.

It was supposed to be bliss, but the sky wasn't bluer, the grass wasn't greener, and I didn't feel like I belonged to something greater in the universe.

Blinded by tears, I dressed and walked home. Avoiding my mother, I went straight to my room. I couldn't bring myself to tell my mother I had trusted someone who didn't care about me at all! How could I tell her I was no longer a virgin? As I climbed the stairs, they squeaked.

"Florence? Is that you?" She came into the hall and stared at me. "Why aren't you in school? Are you all right?"

"I don't feel well."

"Well, go lie down and rest."

I went to my room and put the pillow over my head to muffle the sound of my crying.

I thought sex would be the answer, but sex wasn't love at all.

Chapter 4 | Kissing Frogs

My cousin Lee graduated one year before me. She was going to Miami University in her new yellow Volkswagen Bug, a car I found hideous, but still envied her independence. While she was having adventures in sunny Florida, I was in my last year of high school.

The counselors had already decided my future.

"You're not college material," they told me with certainty, nudging me away from math and science and shoving me into Basic English and electives like Home Economics.

At first, I thought it was great—no homework, no pressure, just empty hours waiting for the bell to ring.

Nothing was expected, and nothing was achieved. Between classes, students stood outside the wings, smoking cigarettes. By then, I was smoking a pack a day with my friends. Sometimes, I cut class and hung out in the *Commons*, a large area where students congregated when they weren't in class.

All my classes were in the morning. The last was P.E., which I tried to avoid and often cut to go home for lunch. No one cared, except for one teacher, Mr. Lieberman, the record-keeping instructor.

When he saw me in the hall with a friend, he came out to lecture me about cutting class. "You're wasting your potential, he said. "You could be great at accounting if you put your mind to it."

Accounting? The thought never crossed my mind, but his belief in me ignited a flicker of confidence. I began to take an interest in school. Around the same time, I had just finished reading *The Lord of the Rings*. I loved the story so much that I sat on my front stoop and wrote a screenplay adaptation.

Feeling hopeful, I signed up for a children's theater class in the second semester and presented the script to my teacher, Mr. Johnson. He barely made it through the first scene before his brows knit together. With a dismissive sigh, he let the pages flutter onto his desk. "This story isn't written for children."

Set back, I had to ask myself, *What am I good at?* The only thing that interested me was music. I'd stay in my room for hours listening to records. *Maybe... music.* I dreamed of playing the piano, but that would be impossible. A piano is expensive, and where would I even practice? *Maybe the guitar.* There was a small music studio just four blocks from my house. Lessons were five dollars an hour.

Determined, I took a part-time job at the pizzeria. Saving every cent until I could afford an old guitar. The first lessons made my fingers sting, but I pushed through and learned to play my first melody, *In the House of the Rising Sun.*

In my final semester of high school, I enrolled in a music theory course. I scheduled an appointment with my school counselor. Mr. Murphy looked over my records and shook his head. "I'm afraid you don't have the required classes you need to apply for college. I had to find another route to independence.

So I went on a mission to find the perfect mate. The search for my prince was daunting as I kissed one frog after another. No prince appeared.

The heat of summer rolled onto Long Island like a gentle wave. Jones Beach was crowded with sun worshipers, their blankets and towels sprawled across the sand.

After a day of sunbathing, I scrambled onto one of the buses in the parking lot and rode home.

When I walked into the kitchen, my mother nodded toward the hall table.

"You got mail today."

I picked up the envelope and carried it to my room. The return address read Private Vincent Santino. Co A 25th Infantry, APO SF 96383.

Vinny?

I tore it open, and a photograph slipped out. He stood in uniform, his black, wavy hair cropped short, still quite handsome. He reminded me of Geraldo Rivera, a journalist on WABC.

Dear Florence,

I hope you remember me. We used to hang around the deli with friends, but we never really spoke. I always thought you were pretty, and I was hoping you might want to write to me while I'm in Vietnam. I get lonely for home. It sure would give me something to look forward to. If you're not spoken for already (I hope you're not!) and if you're not too busy, please send me a short note. Oh, and could you include a picture?

Vinny

I rummaged through my desk drawer for some paper and wrote back immediately.

Dear Vinny,

I was surprised to get your letter. Yes, I remember you. I didn't realize you were drafted into the war. I'm including a photo of me, but I'm not very photogenic.

Florence

Before sealing the envelope, I spritzed it with Youth Dew, a cologne I'd bought at Woolworths down by the train station. Its scent was a blend of cinnamon, cloves, and vanilla.

I walked to the post office and mailed it, imagining him opening it somewhere far away.

Chapter 5 | Letters from Vietnam

Three weeks later, another letter arrived. I flopped onto my bed and read it.

Dear Florence,

You have no idea how much your letter meant to me. I was thrilled when I heard my name called during the mail call. I could smell the perfume even before I opened your letter. In fact, one of the guys grabbed it from me and passed it around so everyone could get a whiff. I showed everyone your picture. They agree that you are quite beautiful.

The sergeant sneered and said that you wouldn't be free by the time I got home. He's such a jerk. I hope he's wrong.

It sounds like you're having a fun summer. I wish I could be there. The beach here is beautiful. On my days off, I enjoy swimming. I almost think I'm on vacation, but that doesn't last long. Soon, it's back to work, long days of hiking, and longer nights eaten by mosquitoes. The jungle is treacherous because the leaves in the bushes are sharp like razors. Sometimes, I don't even know I'm cut until I feel the blood running down my face.

Several days a week, I'm on patrol looking for the VC. They call it a search-and-destroy mission. When we march through the jungle, we have to watch out for booby traps, or we could be blown to smithereens. It sounds worse than it is, but it helps to be able to share it with someone.

Please don't stop writing. I look forward to your letters.

Vinny

Dear Vinny,

I'm sorry to hear about your mission. For me, the worst part would be the mosquitoes. They always seem to seek me out, even if I drench myself in bug spray. I don't know too much about the war, except what I hear on the nightly news, but I'm afraid I haven't been paying attention. I asked my father what the Viet Cong was, and he said they were Communist guerrillas who made surprise attacks. That's awful. I hope you remain safe. I'll keep writing.

Florence

Summer was coming to an end. The ocean water was getting too cold to swim in, and I went to the beach less often. Instead, I hung out at the Mall. My friends and I walked around smoking cigarettes and buying French fries at the food court. We loved window shopping and dreaming of what we would buy if we could. We especially loved the bridal shop and dreamed of what our weddings would be like when we met the right guy.

"Another letter came for you today," my mother said. "I think it's from that boy in Vietnam." She frowned and handed me the envelope.

Dear Florence,

I had a terrible week. I think I'm going to go out of my mind. You don't know what it's like to be constantly watching your back and expecting a bullet to blow you away at any moment. Sorry, I'm sure you don't want to hear about this stuff. You're lucky to be far away from it. I count the days before I can come home. By the way, I had a dream the other night…well, it was really a nightmare. I dreamt that you were seeing another guy. It made me feel so angry. I'm sure men must ask you out all the time. I hope you aren't cheating on me.

XOXO Vinny

I ignored the tight feeling in my chest and hid his letter under my bed.

The war in Vietnam ended, and Vinny was coming home. Almost immediately, his jealousy intensified. At the beach one day, a man whistled as we walked along the boardwalk.

"Cover yourself up," he sneered. "You're attracting attention."

He made me wrap a blanket around my swimsuit in the August heat. I nearly fainted.

"Mark my words, Florence. "A man like that doesn't change. He'll only get worse."

Ignoring my mother's warnings, we were soon engaged.

Among billowing white taffeta cinched at the waist, I clung to my father's arm as we walked down the aisle.

I basked in the attention, floating on the thrill of being Mrs. Vincent Santino. Yet, even as we kissed at the altar, a shadow of doubt lingered.

Our honeymoon was in the Poconos, heart-shaped beds and champagne tubs.

Although many couples' activities were planned, Vinny preferred that we stay to ourselves. The only time we mingled was for dinner in the large dining room. Seated with other couples around the table, I relished the title of newlywed.

I was determined to be the perfect homemaker. At first, it was fun, playing house, cooking dinners, and decorating our one-bedroom apartment.

Vinny didn't like visitors.

Laura and Tim, a young couple, lived in the upstairs apartment. Laura had fiery red hair and an outgoing personality. Every day, her sisters came to visit. Their laughter floated through the halls, a sound so full of life it made me ache with longing.

One day, there was a knock on my door. It was Laura. She asked if I could help her move a piece of furniture in her apartment. From then on, we became good friends.

At first, Vinny tolerated our friendship, but his jealousy surfaced like a black tide. Vinny tightened his grip until I couldn't breathe. I devised a signal to let Laura know it was safe to come down by tapping on the ceiling with a broomstick.

Then, he took a job as a county sanitation worker. He'd leave for work at four each morning and be home by nine am after his route. My only reprieve came in running small errands, like trips to the bank or supermarket.

"What took you so long? Were you shopping or socializing?"

I drank coffee and chain-smoked over a deck of cards playing solitaire. I lost weight. My mother noticed.

When Vinny became careless during sex, I suspected he was trying to get me pregnant, so I lied to get contraception.

"Mom," I whispered into the receiver, being careful Vinny didn't overhear, "Can you pick me up tomorrow. I have a doctor's appointment, and I don't want Vinny to know."

"Where do you intend to tell him you're going?"

"I'll just tell him that you have the appointment and want me to come along."

"You shouldn't have to lie about where you go?" There was concern in her voice.

"Please, Mom. It's easier this way."

❀

One night, after attending a bridal shower, I came home to beer cans and the smell of alcohol.

"Where the hell have you been all night?" he slurred.

"I was at my cousin's bridal shower," I said, but my voice trembled.

"Don't lie to me! A bridal shower doesn't last that long. You couldn't have been there the whole time."

"Were men at this party?"

"No! The shower was for women only."

"For women only," he mocked, his voice laced with venom. "I don't believe that shit for one minute. You made the whole thing up so you could see your lover. Who is he? Tim from upstairs? I see the way he looks at you."

When I rushed to the kitchen phone to call my father. "Dad...."

Vinny ripped the phone cord from the wall.

I rushed into the hall and grabbed the broomstick, screaming for help.

Vinny tore the broom from my hands. I fled into the bathroom and locked the door.

He pounded so hard I feared he would break it down.

After a long period of silence, I dared to come out. Vinny had passed out on the bed, his body sprawled out across the sheets.

There was a knock at the door. It was my father, and he wasn't happy.

"Florence! Get your things. You're coming home! And take off that ring."

I obediently stuffed my belongings into a bag.

"Don't you ever come near my daughter again!" my father threatened.

We drove home in silence. We pulled up in front of the house, and he finally spoke. "He's not about to let you go without a fight."

As my father predicted, Vinny showed up at our small colonial house. Alone in my bedroom, I crouched under the window with my back against the wall.

"I'm sorry!" he cried.

A twinge of pity washed over me. For a moment, I wondered if I should go downstairs and talk to him. Just as I weakened, my father's car pulled into the driveway. Vinny drove off.

Chapter 6 | Pedal to the Metal

One week before the divorce, the phone in the kitchen rang. My mother nodded at me to get it. She was busy making meatballs, her hands slimy with the egg-and-meat mixture.

"Hello?"

"Vinny's at New Island Hospital! He's had an accident."

The voice was cold and flat, as if she were just delivering the news. I pressed the phone against my ear and turned my back to the stereo, which was blasting The Italian Hour.

"What? Who is this?"

But the line had already gone dead.

I stood there, the phone still in my hand. *Accident?* A wave of nausea surged through me.

"I have to go," I said, turning to my mother. "Vinny's in the hospital. Something happened."

"Do you want me to come with you?"

"No, I'll be fine." I wasn't sure if I was lying to her or myself.

The engine of my black Ford Falcon rumbled to life, and I drove toward the hospital. When I finally pulled into the emergency lot, I didn't get out right away. I just sat there, gripping the wheel, trying to control my thoughts. Finally, I forced myself to move.

Inside, the receptionist asked if she could help me.

"I'm here to see Vinny Santino."

Her eyes scanned the admissions registry. "He's in the ICU. Family only."

"I'm his wife."

She looked at my ID and handed me a visitor's pass.

"Fourth floor," she said. "The elevator's down the hall."

The ride up felt like a climb toward something I wasn't ready for. The elevator doors opened with a dull ding. The air was heavy with the scent of disinfectant and feces, mingled with the stench of sickness and death.

The nurses at the station were busy chatting among themselves. The lights on their panel blinked, but they were ignored.

I found Vinny's room and froze in the doorway. The rhythmic hiss of a ventilator filled the air. I peeked inside. He lay still, a plastic tube protruding from his throat, pumping air into his lungs. He looked small and fragile. Nothing like the man I'd married. I moved closer. His eyes opened and met mine. He tried to speak, but I couldn't understand. Vinny's eyes filled with frustration, and the monitor beeped rapidly.

A nurse rushed in.

"What happened to him?" I asked.

"Pool accident. He dove into the shallow end and sustained spinal trauma. He's paralyzed from the waist down."

Paralyzed?

The word echoed in my mind. The divorce hearing was a week away. I was about to end our marriage. *How could I now? What would people say? What kind of woman leaves her husband like this?*

Vinny stared at me with pleading eyes. *Don't leave me,* they begged.

I reached for his hand. "Don't worry. I'll take care of you."

At that moment, I meant it.

The intercom crackled. "Visiting hours end in fifteen minutes."

"I'll be back in the morning," I said gently.

But before I could move, the door burst open, and his mother swept in like a storm. "What are you doing here?" Gloria shouted.

The alarm went off as Vinny's heart rate spiked.

"I'm here, Sonny," she cooed. "Mama's here."

The nurse returned, checked the machines, and scribbled some notes. "Please keep him calm," she said, leaving me alone with Vinny's mother.

Gloria's eyes blazed. "You did this! she screamed. "My son is paralyzed — because of you."

I turned to leave, but she came after me. I rushed toward the elevator and slammed the down button with my palm. When the doors opened, I jumped inside, but just as they were about to close, Gloria shoved her way in. I was trapped. Accusations spewed from her mouth like daggers.

The ride down seemed like an eternity. When the doors finally opened, I bolted out of the elevator, through the ER doors, and across the parking lot. I didn't stop until I reached my car.

Only then did I exhale the breath I'd been holding and let it out. My hands trembled as I turned the key in the engine.

My parents paid the Catholic Church one thousand dollars to have the marriage annulled.

Chapter 7 | Dippy Girl

My father agreed to set up a tiny studio apartment for me in the basement. It was mine. My own space. A little world tucked away beneath the house. In the combined living room/bedroom, a gas fire flickered in the fireplace my father had made from scraps of marble. Its glow cast restless shadows on the walls. The kitchen/dining area barely fit a small stove, sink, and refrigerator, and in the corner by the door stood a lonely wooden table. The bathroom? Smaller than the closet upstairs, just big enough for a cramped shower stall, a sink, and a toilet.

It felt like a Hobbit's house. Cozy, small, and full of possibility.

Now that I had my own place, I needed a job, but without transportation, I was stuck.

My father's truck was still parked in the driveway, indicating he hadn't left for work yet. He sat in the kitchen drinking a cup of coffee. I could tell his mind was elsewhere. His tousled brown hair gave him a boyish look.

"Dad, will you teach me to drive when you get home from work?"

"You don't have a driver's permit."

"Oh."

He sighed. "I'll take you to get your driver's permit when I get home, but I won't be able to take you out for a lesson until the weekend."

"Thanks, Dad."

He didn't respond, just disappeared into the bedroom. A few minutes later, he reappeared in his blue county uniform. I noted that he was still a handsome man and in good shape for his age. *Maybe that's why my mother fell in love with him.*

"By the way," he asked. "Where's your mother?"

"She's probably at Bingo!"

He smirked, grabbed his car keys, and went out the front door.

Bingo was a sore spot for him.

That weekend, I gripped a steering wheel for the first time. My father promised I could have his car if I passed the driver's test. It was an ugly black Ford Falcon and smelled like motor oil and aftershave, but it ran. That was all that mattered. The thought of having a license in my wallet and car keys in my hand sent a thrill through me.

A few weeks later, I was driving. My uncle pulled some strings and got me a job at the aerospace corporation where he worked.

On my first day, I drove through the massive gates, hands clammy on the steering wheel. The guard at the station gave me a pass with my name and directed me to Plant Three.

Inside the front lobby, a woman sat behind the reception desk. Her hair was high, her eyes etched with thick black eyeliner.

"Today is my first day," I said, and slid my work assignment papers toward her.

She tapped at the computer, her long fingernails hammering away at the keys. Then she looked up.

"Have a seat. I'll call someone to escort you to your department."

A few minutes later, a young woman around my age pushed through the double doors. She had a confident air, the kind that came from knowing exactly where she fit in this world.

"Hi, I'm Joanne," she said with a grin. "I'm the head Dippy Girl."

"Dippy Girl?"

She laughed. "That's what they call us. It stands for data input processing."

Stepping through the double doors, we entered a large warehouse. The air was thick with the scent of jet fuel, and somewhere in the distance, the deep rumble of a fighter plane growled. It shook the building. The sound grew louder as we turned the corner, and suddenly, I saw it—an F-14, sleek and magnificent, gleaming under the overhead lights. I stopped in my tracks, overwhelmed by the sights, the sounds, the sheer power of it all. I felt like I had entered another world.

The steady hum of industry surrounded me as we entered the mechanical department. Drills whirled. Machinery clanked. Rows of long workbenches filled the room, reminding me of a high school science lab. Men — some young, most old enough to be my father — were hunched over their stations, soldering metal or working with electronic boards. Not a single woman worked on the floor.

A voice called out.

"Hey! We got a new Dippy Girl!"

Heads turned, and a few workers grinned as Joanne led me to a computer. Beside it sat a cart filled with aircraft parts, each wrapped in plastic and labeled with a code.

"The red cart is for incoming. The blue cart is for outgoing," Joanne explained. "You'll enter each part and serial number into the system. Once you get the hang of it, I'll train you in the electrical department." She smirked. "Oh, and if you ever run out of work, come find me in the ladies' room."

I raised an eyebrow.

"That's where all the Dippy girls hang out and talk office politics," she said with a wink. "You know — who's dating who, who's cheating on their wife…"

I forced a smile but kept my thoughts to myself. I wanted to fit in with the other girls, but petty gossip had never interested me. I wasn't sure where I fit in yet, but one thing was certain — I had no intention of joining Joanne's little clique in the ladies' room.

I was working. I was driving. I had my own space. Maybe, just maybe, that was enough.

Chapter 8 | Amphibians
1974

One morning, I glanced into the shop at work and saw a handsome new employee at his bench. His name was Keith—fair-skinned, dirty blond hair, and a twinkle in his eyes that made me melt. I started walking past his station every day, pretending it was coincidental, hoping he'd notice. It became a ritual until one morning, he finally started a conversation. Soon after, he asked me out.

It was October. Leaves blazed in the trees as we walked through the park, and at night, the stars looked close enough to touch. We fell in love to the background hum of *I Only Have Eyes for You.*

By Christmas, all signs pointed to an engagement. I arrived at his house in a forest green jumpsuit, balancing a ten-pound basket of Italian Butter Cookies. His father was German, his mother was Irish, and I couldn't shake the feeling that they didn't approve of him dating an Italian girl. They tried to make me feel welcome, but I didn't. Still, I shook it off. Gifts waited under the tree, and my eyes locked on a small red box with a silver bow. The tag had my name on it. I was sure it contained jewelry — A *ring!*

"It's snowing!" one of the kids shouted, and we all rushed outside. For a moment, everything felt magical.

At midnight, we gathered around the tree. When it was my turn, I tore open the wrapping and opened the red velvet box. All eyes were on me as disappointment flashed over my face, but I forced a smile. *Earrings!*

Disappointment flashed across my face before I could hide it. I forced a smile.

"Do you like them?" Keith asked.

"I love them," I lied, replacing my gold hoops with the ruby studs.

Later, I overheard a cousin whisper that I looked like a lady of the evening. I didn't understand the phrase, but I understood the tone. I retreated to the corner beside the cookie basket and ate one after another as if it might fill the ache.

By the end of the evening, my jumpsuit felt too tight. Then, as if the universe wanted to finish the job, I bent down, and the back seam split. It was the worst Christmas of my life.

Thank goodness for my friend Cindy. Every weekend, we woke up early to play tennis. Sometimes, we used the country club tennis courts, pretending we belonged there and hoping Mr. Right would wander into the next set.

"Maybe we should go clubbing," Cindy suggested.

Neither of us danced. Neither of us drank. Still, we decided to give it a shot.

On a balmy summer night, we made our grand entrance into a swanky place dressed in our sexiest outfits. We sashayed into the dimly lit bar and followed the music, heads held high, until we missed the step up and landed face-first on the carpet.

Damn heels! We scrambled to our feet and left as fast as we could, hoping no one had seen.

Outside, we burst out in hysterical laughter. Unfortunately, the event didn't go without an audience. Two guys came running after us to make sure we were okay. It took a while to convince them we were fine and get away.

We escaped to our favorite hangout — the Nautilus Diner on Merrick Road, where our dignity could be restored over a hot cup of coffee and a corn muffin.

"If we want to meet someone decent," I said, we need to broaden our horizons.

Cindy swore European men were more romantic. After another failed attempt to find love, I let her convince me to take a trip to Europe to visit her great-uncle in Copenhagen.

With our passports and bags, Cindy and I proceeded through airport security. Most of the passengers on our FinAir flight were Scandinavian, with icy blue eyes and blonde hair. My Mediterranean complexion stood out in the sea of pale faces.

Damark was charming and strange. Cindy's uncle welcomed us into his modest home. The bathroom had no shower, just a tub with a spray attachment, and the toilet flushed with a dangling cord you pulled like a bell.

Once we settled in, the family took us to Tivoli Park, the second-oldest amusement park in the world. Copenhagen glittered under lights. Violin music floated through the air. Children laughed at a puppet show. Couples held hands as they walked along the street, and I wondered what it would be like to fall in love beneath the stars of Europe.

Each morning, Cindy's uncle returned from the bakery with fresh rolls and pastries that melted in our mouths. It felt like they fed us six meals a day. We had no complaints—except for the skinless cucumbers that kept appearing at every meal, turning green around the edges.

We saw the famous Little Mermaid statue, ducked into ancient churches, and wandered through museums until our feet ached. It was a strange and wonderful culture.

I convinced Cindy that we should go to England and France, and her uncle made the arrangements.

Like the typical tourists, we thought that London would welcome us. After all, we spoke the same language. But their accents were thick, and we found ourselves nodding politely through conversations we barely understood. Still, we enjoyed riding the London Underground and taking pictures in front of Big Ben.

Paris was next. Ever since Elementary school, when I had a brief lesson in French, I was captivated by the language.

Arriving in Paris, we found a café on a corner in the 7th arrondissement, soaking up the culture, and sipping cappuccinos, blissfully unaware that it was a drink reserved for breakfast in Europe.

Lost in our Americanized babble, we didn't notice the young man across the café watching—until he appeared at our table, holding his tasse de café. Very French and strikingly handsome.

"Je m'appelle André. Puis-je te rejoinder?" he asked, pulling out a chair before we could answer.

We glanced at each other, and Cindy smiled. Not knowing much French, we struggled to understand him. We pulled out our French-English dictionary and attempted some awkward phrases.

With a trace of irritation, André gestured boldly. "Why you no speak French?" He groaned dramatically and laughed. "Pas plus!"

We all laughed, and in broken English, he teased us for American manners, then forgave our innocence.

André took an instant liking to Cindy. She flirted with ease, tossing her hair and laughing at all the right moments.

We finished our cappuccinos and over-tipped our waiter, not realizing that it was already included.

As we strolled the cobblestone streets of Paris, André pointed out monuments and cafés he thought we should visit.

"I have apartment… with a view of … the Eiffel Tower," he said. "Aimerais tu le voir?"

Cindy and I exchanged a look and made a silent telepathic decision. We didn't think twice about the danger. This was Paris, after all. Adventure was part of the plan.

His building was old. The elevator was narrow. It barely fit all three of us. On the seventh floor, he opened the door to a small apartment with enormous windows and a breathtaking view of the Eiffel Tower.

André put a record on the turntable, and we stepped out onto the balcony. Music drifted into the night. The city glowed.

Then I realized I was alone.

I followed the sound of voices to the back room and stopped short. Cindy and André were tangled together in his bed.

"Sorry," I muttered, backing away.

All I wanted was out. I reached for the doorknob just as Cindy appeared behind me. "Don't leave," she said, unsure.

"It's fine," I said quickly. "Just make sure he gets you back to the hotel in one piece."

I stepped into the elevator and headed down to the city streets, jealousy simmering under my skin. Of course, he wanted Cindy — blonde, blue-eyed, effortless.

I walked aimlessly, unsure if I should wait at a café or go back to the hotel. Minutes later, I heard quick footsteps behind me.

"I'm so sorry!" Cindy cried, tears running down her cheeks. "I didn't mean for that to happen."

"It's okay," I said, forcing a laugh. "I probably wouldn't have said no either—even if it was me he wanted."

We walked toward our hotel, together, the Eiffel Tower glowing behind us, music drifting into the Paris warm night.

Then André came running after us, breathless.

"Filles, s'il vous plait," he said." Je veux vous deux... ménage à trois.

Cindy and I stared at each other, then burst out laughing.

André's face hardened. He turned on his heel and stomped away, murmuring French obscenities we didn't need a dictionary to understand.

Once he was out of sight, we laughed again. Just another frog—this one with a French accent.

Chapter 9 | Croaker

1978

A long, cold Long Island winter kept me hibernating in my apartment. Snow flurries fell throughout the night like a silent lullaby until the rumble of snowplows woke me in the morning. I dressed slowly, dragging myself upstairs to have a cup of coffee with my mother—a morning ritual. My sister Julia was already at work, and Carol was in school.

She was sitting alone in the kitchen. She jumped up to pour me a cup of coffee.

I sighed and sat down.

"I've noticed you've been staying home a lot lately," she said. "Mr. Right's not going to knock on your door, you know."

I rolled my eyes. I'd heard it before. "Mom, I wouldn't know Mr. Right if I met him.

We had the same conversation every day. I checked the clock. "I have to go to work, Mom." I gave her a quick hug and left.

After work, I stopped for Chinese take-out and rushed home, looking forward to a quiet night in. I wasn't expecting visitors, but before I could plunge the chopsticks into my shrimp chow mein, a knock at the door interrupted my meal. *Who could that be?*

Peeking through the curtain, I saw a young man in faded blue jeans and a shabby army jacket standing outside. His long hair hung down to his shoulders, topped with a knitted ski cap. He looked oddly familiar. Reluctantly, I opened the door a crack, and a blast of icy air slipped inside, making me shiver.

"Remember me?"

I studied his face. "Oh, yeah. Michael Corrigan! I went to school with your younger brother. You live on Maple Street, right?"

"Yeah. I'm home for a little while, visiting my parents. I remembered you lived a few blocks away."

"Home? Where've you been?"

"Ohio. I wasn't ready to rejoin civilization when I was discharged from the army, so I moved there. There were fewer people. Easier." He stepped inside and glanced around my apartment. "Hey, I have some good pot. Do you smoke?"

"No," I said, *Why did I open the door?*

"In Vietnam, it was easier to get than cigarettes," he added with a lopsided grin.

I tried steering the conversation to a different subject. "Will you be in town long?"

"Not sure. I don't like Long Island."

"Oh. Well, I was getting ready to eat dinner."

"Okay. I have to visit a friend I haven't seen in a while. Maybe we can hang out sometime."

"Sure, maybe," I said, thinking that would get rid of him.

I heard him take off on his motorcycle and thought, *How could anyone not like Long Island?*

Another ten inches of snow had fallen by morning. I curled up with a book for the day.

Later that afternoon, a knock came at the door. Peering through the frosted window, I saw him again—Michael. I stepped back, but it was too late. He had already caught sight of me. I opened the door.

"How did you get here?" I asked.

He brushed snow off his jacket and smiled as if it were no big deal. "I have a tow truck. A buddy hooked me up with a job rescuing stranded drivers. I'll be riding all night. Wanna come along?"

"Are you crazy? It's freezing out there."

"Layer up. You'll have fun, I promise."

I sighed. "All right, but I don't want to get stuck on some desolate road."

"Don't worry. You're safe with me."

"I might hold you to that."

The snow crunched beneath my boots as I climbed into the cab of his truck. My breath fogged in the frigid air.

We drove through the night, sliding on the icy roads and laughing. We shared stories and helped drivers who were trapped in their vehicles.

Before he dropped me off, he asked if he could call me.

Chapter 10 | Winter Thaw

The frozen roads turned into slush, and the late-night coffees stretched longer.

By early April, we were inseparable. I went upstairs to have coffee with my mother. The sun streamed through the double glass doors in the dining room, casting a warm glow over the kitchen.

My mother sat at the table, eating an Entenmann's cheese Danish. Just the sight of it twisted my stomach into knots.

She looked up with a smile in her eyes. "Good morning. There's fresh coffee on the stove. I'll pour you a cup."

"I can get it," I said, beating her to the stove. I sat across from her with my coffee and reached for the milk. Steam rose as I took a sip. I tried to force a smile but failed.

"Are you all right, Florence? You look a little pale."

"Yes... uh... no." My voice cracked, and a lump formed in my throat. My fingers nervously twisted the worn cover of a matchbook.

Tears welled in my eyes. "Mom, I need to talk to you about something."

Her smile faltered, replaced by a look of concern. "What's wrong?"

"Michael asked me to marry him." The words tumbled out.

Her eyes widened slightly. "Oh. And what did you say?"

"I... I haven't given him an answer yet," I confessed, my voice trembling with uncertainty. "I'm not sure if I love him."

She reached across the table, placing a gentle hand on mine. "Love is complicated. It's not always clear-cut, especially when you're young. You're only twenty-two. You have plenty of time to figure things out. There's no need to rush into marriage if you're uncertain."

My heart hammered. I stared at my trembling hands, unable to meet her gaze.

"Mom," I said, my voice breaking. "I... I'm pregnant."

She blinked, stunned, then slowly lowered herself into the nearest chair.

"Pregnant?" she repeated, the word hanging in the air between us. "Are you sure?"

I nodded, my eyes fixed on the floor.

She sighed and rubbed her temples like she was trying to press the news into a place she could manage. "You're so young," she said, her voice tight with worry. "This isn't the life I wanted for you."

I pressed my lips together and nodded, staring at the edge of the table.

Then she looked at me — really looked at me — and something in her face softened. "But what's done is done. We'll get through it. You're not alone."

I nodded again. My eyes blurred, and I focused on the pattern in the linoleum until it steadied. I wasn't sure if I believed her, but in that moment, I needed to.

I rested my palm against my stomach and felt its unfamiliar curve.

Later that day, I told Michael. He grinned and pulled me into a tight embrace.

"I'm so happy," he said. "We're going to be a family."

The unwavering optimism in his voice gave me hope. I wasn't alone anymore.

"Let's get married in Ohio," he said a few days later. "My friends live there. We can stay with a teacher I know — he and his wife have a log cabin. You'll love it."

A flicker of curiosity stirred inside me. I'd never been to Ohio. I'd barely left New York, except for a weekend trip to a resort in Pennsylvania.

"All right," I said. "Let's do it."

We packed up my Camaro and drove west. The wedding was nothing like my first — no gown, no flowers, no music. I wore a bell-sleeved shirt and gaucho pants. Michael's best friend and his wife stood up for us. They came back to the cabin and cooked dinner for all of us, their warmth filling in the blanks where tradition had been.

When we returned home, Michael started looking for work. My belly was already showing. Each day, I spent time with my mother. We talked about the baby over tuna sandwiches and cups of coffee.

We sat across from each other for hours, our coffee cups empty. This would be her first grandchild, and I felt her quiet pride glowing around me like sunlight.

At just six weeks, the heartburn was already brutal.

"That's a sign you're having a girl," she chirped, smiling.

I imagined a tiny pink dress, satin booties. My days were filled with doctor's visits, shopping for baby clothes with my mother, and making plans.

So when Michael said he wanted to move to Texas, it felt like the floor dropped out beneath me.

"The housing market's booming," he said. "I could get a job on a construction crew with your brother."

The idea of living closer to my brother wasn't terrible, but I didn't want to leave Long Island. I didn't want to leave *her*.

"My mom's excited about the baby! I can't just leave."

"You can come back to visit anytime you want," he replied casually, like it was no big deal.

I nodded without speaking.

We loaded up the car and hitched a trailer for his motorcycle. After a tearful goodbye, I kissed my parents, and we hit the road.

We stopped at campgrounds and state parks along the way. Michael loved the open sky. "It makes me feel safe," he said.

Pregnancy didn't agree with me. Morning sickness was a lie—it hit morning, noon, and night. By the time we arrived at each stop, I was too nauseated to do much more than collapse on the small pool float Michael bought for me. My back ached, and my energy drained away day by day. I missed my bed. But mostly, I missed my mother.

It was dark when we finally arrived in Houston. Palm trees shimmered under the streetlights, swaying gently in the warm air. We found the furnished apartment and settled in for the night.

By morning, sunlight spilled through the blinds, casting a golden glow across the carpet. The clouds hung low. I could almost reach out and touch them. I wandered outside to check out the clubhouse and pool—it looked like something out of a vacation brochure.

Still, Houston felt like another world. Cowboy hats. Pickup trucks with rifles in the back windows. People who smiled with their mouths but not their eyes. I tried to picture myself fitting in here.

I wasn't sure I could.

Chapter 11 | Yellow Satin

When I felt the first kicks of life inside me, I burst into tears of joy. The nausea eased, but a hollow ache settled in its place. In the morning, I pictured my mother's kitchen, the clinking of cups, and the smell of coffee.

Michael liked to joke that he was a New Yorker who'd finally escaped, but to me, it felt like I'd been kidnapped and dropped into someone else's dream.

Houston was suffocatingly hot—a sticky, relentless heat I'd never known back in New York. Each doctor's appointment reminded me I'd be delivering my baby among strangers. The baby moved and stretched inside me. It was the only part of pregnancy I truly loved.

Michael took whatever job he could get, learning as he went, but never complained, even if it meant sweating on hot tar roofs all day. With a baby on the way, he cut his hair and sold his motorcycle. He shrugged it off, but I knew better.

Living in his friend's spare room was difficult, but we finally scraped together enough for our own place.

I walked down the street to a small real estate office, my hands pressed protectively over my belly.

Sandra Wilson looked like she'd stepped out of a catalog for southern ladies—forties, big, teased hair, heavy lip liner. *If that's what it takes to have a career, maybe I'm okay with staying home.*

"Can I help you?" she asked.

"I'm looking for an apartment," I said, pressing my hands over my round belly.

"You're in luck. Some new garden units just opened up nearby. I can show you now if you like."

"That would be great."

Sandra grabbed a set of keys from the pegboard, and we headed out in her car.

The first apartment was bright and beautiful, but it was upstairs. I imagined myself dragging a stroller and a baby up those steps every day. It wasn't going to work.

"Do you have anything on the first floor?" I asked, tugging Michael's oversized T-shirt over the top of my unzipped jeans.

She nodded. "Yes, but it's not in this building."

The next unit was darker and cooler, but not in a good way. As Sandra flipped on the lights, huge black bugs scattered all around.

"Roaches!" I shrieked.

"Tree roaches," she said with a laugh. "Welcome to Houston. Don't worry—maintenance can spray."

I imagined the chemicals my baby would breathe. "No, thanks. It's too dark anyway."

"There's one more. It needs a bit of work—paint and carpet cleaning—, but it has a den off the living room. Technically, a one-bedroom, but the extra space might suit you."

We passed the pool and laundry room, then stepped into the last apartment. As soon as we walked in, something clicked.

"Oh, I like this one!"

Sandra smiled. "I thought you might. You could turn the den into a nursery."

"Yes. It's perfect."

"I'll hold it for you with a deposit. Let's head back and get the paperwork started."

"I found an apartment!" When Michael came through the door at the end of the day, I practically shouted.

"I found an apartment today. It has everything— new kitchen appliances, a big bedroom, and a sunny den for the baby—"

"Can this wait until I take a shower?"

"Oh… sure," I said, my excitement draining. "I just couldn't wait to tell you."

"How much is the rent?"

"Five seventy-five."

"Wow. That's steep for a one-bedroom."

"But the den makes it almost like two. We can use it for the baby's room."

"You realize we don't have any furniture, right?"

"We'll buy things piece by piece. We'll start with the basics and sleep on the floor if we have to."

"I thought you were done with camping?"

"We still have the air mattress," I said, rubbing my aching back.

We moved into our own apartment with just a TV, a garage-sale recliner, an air mattress, and four boxes of clothes. I bought a crib on layaway for the baby's room and a used sewing machine.

My first project was a wall hanging I found in *Parents Magazine*—two crescent moons and six stars, all cut from yellow satin and stuffed with batting. I stitched them together and suspended each one on a ribbon. When I hung them on the wall, I stepped back and admired my handicraft.

Throwing myself into motherhood, I sewed curtains and tiny outfits on my machine, all in full-on Susie Homemaker mode. I even made the baby an outfit using a zebra print sheet. It looked ridiculous, but I thought it was adorable.

As long as I was busy, the ache stayed quiet.

Michael moved us to a different apartment every six months to avoid a rent increase. The boxes never stayed unpacked for long.

One evening, he announced we were moving to Ohio. He talked about old friends from college who could help him get started. I traced the distance on a map—one long day from New York. Anything had to feel better than Texas.

He rented a U-Haul, and we piled in with everything we owned. At only six months old,

Annmarie was strapped into her car seat and oblivious to the move. We camped along the way. It wasn't easy with a toddler, but at least the temperature was cooler than Texas.

When we arrived, Michael made arrangements to rent an old house on the outskirts of town. No one had lived there in years. The big picture window in the living room was so grimy I had to use a whole bottle of Windex just to let the light in. The toilet had a stubborn brown ring. I didn't trust the tap water, so I boiled it and filled old milk jugs with the boiled water. The windows were painted shut, and there was no air conditioning. But I told myself, 'Make it work.'

I spent days scrubbing the refrigerator and stove. The baby's room was dark, lit by a bare bulb. Michael hummed as he brought in our furniture, but all I could think about was how close my parents were now. I begged them to visit. And they did.

My mother gasped when she saw how thin I'd gotten, but Annmarie quickly stole her attention. My father took one look at the house and frowned.

"This is just temporary until Michael finds a job," I said quickly.

"You're out in the boonies," he replied. "There are no jobs out here."

Three weeks passed without a single interview. Each morning ended the same way — no call, no leads. Our savings evaporated. We packed the car and headed back to Houston.

Chapter 12 | Young Republicans

Somewhere along the journey back to Texas, I became pregnant again. This time felt different. My body moved through the days with a steadiness I hadn't known before.

Jason was born, and Annmarie had a brother. Eighteen months apart—two car seats, two cribs, and an apartment that was suddenly too small.

I started looking for a house. Every listing I circled came with a price that was out of our reach, so we widened the search and drove north toward the rural stretches to a sleepy little town an hour from the city.

Because Michael was a veteran, we applied for a VA mortgage with no down payment.

We walked through one fixer-upper after another house, each one needing more repairs than the last. My excitement dimmed with each broken window and leaning porch. Just when I was ready to give up, the agent mentioned Jim Walter's Homes—low-cost, prefabricated houses raised on blocks due to flood zones. I cringed at the thought, but curiosity pushed us forward. We drove another fifteen minutes to a tiny place called Cooper.

The house took me by surprise. It was clean, bright, and modern. I wanted it, but the concrete blocks beneath it gave me pause. Still, I crouched beside the vinyl siding that stopped a foot above the ground and studied it like a puzzle.

A week later, we signed the papers. It wasn't a dream home, but it was mine. I could paint the walls any color I liked. I could dig in the garden, cook in my own kitchen, and finally breathe. I went to the pound and picked up a white poodle for the kids. We named him Puff.

Most days began with one child on my hip and the other tugging at my leg.

Michael went off to work. I stayed home, cooking, cleaning, and raising babies. And then—suddenly—I feared I might be pregnant again.

"No," I whispered in horror one morning, hunched over the toilet as my breakfast came up. A week of nausea sent me spiraling. But it was a false alarm. I dropped to my knees in relief. "Thank you, thank you, thank you," I whispered to the heavens.

That scare made Michael agree to a vasectomy without much protest. Romance faded into something quiet and practical. We were kind to each other, but we no longer kissed. I showed love in the only other way I knew how—baking cakes, cookies, and pies. The sweet smell of sugar and spice filled the kitchen. Michael and the kids devoured it all. Baking kept my hands busy when my mind couldn't rest.

We celebrated holidays, hosted relatives from back home, and filled the house with laughter and chatter.

I hosted barbecues and cooked whole chickens and thick slabs of beef on the smoker. My brother and his friends would gather in the backyard.

When we didn't have company on the weekends, we'd load up the car and head to Galveston, camping on the sand and falling asleep to the sound of the waves.

My children seemed happy, but every night, I lay awake, wishing for my mother and aching for home. I wanted to go back to Long Island.

I wondered if my father could help. Maybe he could find Michael a job in the county. I called him — not to ask, but to beg.

"I can get him a job," my father said slowly. "But he'll have to cut his hair and join the Republican Club."

We sold the house through a mortgage assumption and handed over the keys. The new owners then gave us $10,000 to take over the debt. It wasn't much. We lost the VA loan. We lost the equity, but I didn't care. I was going home.

We packed our lives into a U-Haul and headed north, dragging memories behind us like a heavy trailer. Jason, only two and a half, fussed in the back, his little legs kicking against his car seat in protest. Annmarie, now four, was restless—hungry one minute, desperate to go potty the next. Puff, our white poodle, needed a break, too, so we pulled into rest stops as needed, stretching our legs and trying to keep the children calm.

Still, nothing could sour my mood. I rolled the window down and let the air hit my face. Every mile took us closer to home, to my mother, to something familiar. I could almost taste the salt of the Long Island air, even though we were still states away.

By dusk, we reached a roadside motel north of Richmond, Virginia. The neon sign flickered, casting a tired glow on the cracked pavement. The room smelled like mildew and old cigarettes, and even in the dim light, I could see stains on the carpet. But we were too exhausted to be choosy. I double-locked the door, pulled the heavy curtains closed, and unpacked the greasy hamburgers we'd grabbed from a drive-through.

We sat on the edge of the bed, the kids cross-legged on the floor with their fast-food bags, and tried to pretend it was a little picnic. Outside, the roar of semi-trucks on the highway pulsed through the walls like a heartbeat. Sleep was nearly impossible. Every rumble shook the headboard, and the headlights from semi-trucks shone through the windows.

At the first glimmer of dawn, I rose, bleary-eyed. The children were groggy but eager to get going. As we passed through the tiny hotel lobby, Annmarie tugged on my hand.

"Can we have breakfast?" she asked, her big eyes landing on the small buffet of cereal boxes and stale pastries.

"All right," I said gently, brushing her hair behind her ear. "But let's eat fast. I want to get to New York today."

We sat at a rickety table as the kids munched on Cheerios, content in the small pleasure of something sweet and familiar. I stirred powdered creamer into a cup of bitter coffee and stared into it, trying to will away the fatigue behind my eyes.

Michael, looking equally worn, rubbed his temples. "Could you take over some of the driving?" he asked, his voice low and tentative.

I hesitated, not because I didn't want to help, but because I was running on fumes. Still, I nodded. "Of course."

The road stretched ahead like a ribbon, unraveling everything we'd left behind. I gripped the wheel as the speeding traffic zoomed past me. My anxiety was on high alert, mingled with excitement. I kept my eyes on the white lines flashing beneath the tires and didn't look back.

A few hours later, we crossed the Verrazano-Narrows Bridge. Trying to keep up with the rushing traffic, I accelerated, maneuvering past semi-trucks and speeding cars that swerved in front of me. I wasn't used to the traffic whizzing past me and kept my eyes glued to the road. We passed a large body of water on the right, and I saw people fishing, skating, and walking along the sidewalk. My eyes wanted to linger, but I couldn't take them off the road.

When we came to the Southern State Parkway, the traffic eased up, and I relaxed my grip on the wheel.

The familiar scent of salty air hit me, and I breathed in deeply. Being back felt good. When the air turned salty, I breathed in until my chest loosened. The sun sank below the horizon as I admired the majestic old trees lining the roadside. A familiar sign told me I wasn't far from my childhood home, and soon, I took the exit I used to dream of escaping.

We pulled up in front of my family's home, and my mother stood on the stoop. Annmarie ran into her arms. Inside, the living room looked exactly the same as it had for the past fifteen years, down to the gold sectional couch she'd bought from a little furniture store in town. It still looked new under its old plastic cover — untouched by time. I remembered why I'd always hated that thing. In summer, it stuck to your bare legs like cling wrap. I followed the scent of freshly brewed coffee into the kitchen, which seemed smaller than I had remembered.

Exhausted from the trip, Michael and the kids went to bed while I joined my mother in the kitchen for cake and coffee. She confided that she and my father were having marital problems. I had grown accustomed to their war dance. It never dawned on me that it could change, but their marriage was disintegrating since my siblings and I left home. Without us, the house had started to shift.

Chapter 13 | Almost Home

Michael had left for his job interview while the children and I sat around the breakfast table with my mother.

"What are you going to do today?" she asked.

"I think I'll go visiting. I haven't seen Laura in a while. You remember her — the girl who lived upstairs from me when I was married to Vinny?"

"Oh yes," she said, nodding. "I heard she went back to school for her nursing degree."

"Wow, that's great," I said, forcing a smile.

I picked up the phone to call her, but she didn't answer, so I left a message and tried to think of something else to do.

"Let's bring some bread to the lake and feed the ducks," I told the kids.

Autumn was unfurling its tapestry of colors. The air carried a crisp edge that nipped at our cheeks, a silent herald of winter's approach. Leaves drifted lazily from the trees, swirling like golden confetti in a whimsical breeze. A faint, smoky aroma of burning leaves mingled with the earthy scent of damp soil, tugging at memories of childhood. Maple trees flared in shades of burnt orange and scarlet, while the deep purples of ash mingled with the buttery yellows of poplar, creating a vivid, living quilt that painted the landscape. I had forgotten how alive the northern fall could feel, each hue sharper and more vibrant than in Houston's subdued greens and browns.

When we reached the old fence, we slipped silently into the woods, the crunch of leaves beneath our feet breaking the stillness.

"It's so pretty here," Annmarie whispered, her voice full of wonder, her eyes wide as they soaked in the towering canopy above.

"Wait until you see the lake, kids," I said with a smile. "You'll love it."

The deeper we ventured, the dimmer the sunlight became, filtered through the thick lattice of branches overhead. The air turned cooler, tinged with the faint musk of moss and decaying leaves. Jason clutched my hand tightly, his small fingers trembling.

"I'm scared," he murmured, his voice barely audible over the rustle of the forest.

"There's nothing to be afraid of, sweetheart," I said, kneeling to meet his wide, uncertain eyes. "When I was your age, I came here all the time. It's magical."

I bent down and turned over a mossy log, hoping to reveal a darting salamander or the glimmer of a garter snake's scales. Instead, a frenzy of ants erupted, their tiny legs scrambling in chaos as they cradled pale eggs, desperate to shield them from the sudden intrusion.

At last, we stepped into the clearing, and the sight before us sucked the breath from my lungs. Where I had expected the glimmer of water rippling in the afternoon sun, I saw only a desolate expanse. The lake was gone, replaced by a muddy, stagnant swamp. The air hung heavy with the sour stench of decay, thick and oppressive. The silence was unnerving — no chorus of frogs, no splash of ducks landing on water. Only the faint hum of insects broke the stillness.

"Yuck!" Annmarie exclaimed, scrunching her nose in disgust. "Where's the lake?"

"I guess it dried up," I said softly, my voice hollow with disbelief. "Or maybe… maybe we took a wrong turn."

High above us, the sky seemed endless, vast, and pale. A flock of ducks passed in elegant formation, their wings whispering against the heavens as they moved southward. Their absence only deepened the emptiness around us. Shadows stretched long and cold across the open field as the sun dipped lower, its warmth fading with the day.

"Can we leave now, Mommy?" Jason's voice quivered, and his small hand tugged on mine. His blue eyes brimmed with tears, threatening to spill over, reflecting the muted light of the overcast sky.

"Yes, sweetheart. I think we've seen enough," I said, my heart heavy as I turned us away from the swamp. The woods seemed darker as we retraced our steps, the weight of disappointment clinging to the air like a shroud.

We returned to the house, subdued. As I walked into the kitchen, the phone was ringing.

"Oh, here she is now," my mother said, handing it to me. "It's your friend, Laura."

"Hello?"

"Hi, Florence! I don't have to work today. I was wondering if you and the kids wanted to come over."

"We'd love to! Are you still living in the apartment?"

"No, Tim and I bought a house."

"That's wonderful!"

I jotted down her new address and stopped at the bakery for some of our favorite pastries. When we arrived, the cobblestone walkway was lined with cheerful red and pink begonias. I could already hear children playing inside.

Laura opened the door with her six-month-old on her hip. Her older daughter, Beth, peeked shyly from behind her, and her five-year-old son grinned when he saw me.

"Do you want to see my toys?" Beth asked Annmarie and Jason. They nodded and dashed off to the bedroom. I followed Laura into the kitchen.

"Coffee?" she offered.

"I'd love some," I said, holding out the little white box.

"You didn't!" Her eyes lit up. "Are those the cream-filled cakes we used to devour at the apartment?"

She tore open the box, grinning. "I really shouldn't," she laughed, patting her stomach. "I still haven't lost the baby weight."

"You look fine to me. I still can't believe you are a nurse," I said, smiling.

"Yeah, right? I used to faint at the sight of blood, remember? But I love it now. Staying home was fine for a while, but I needed something more, so I went back to school."

"I've thought about going back, too. I just don't know what I want to study."

Jason came running into the kitchen. "Beth and Annmarie are fighting."

"What now?" Laura sighed.

"Annmarie has my doll and won't give it back!" Beth called from the hallway.

"Can't you share?" Laura asked.

"No, I want her to leave!"

Embarrassed, Laura walked off to settle things. A few minutes later, Beth returned with a muttered apology, but the mood had shifted.

I could feel it—we weren't the same anymore. Whatever thread had once tied us together had frayed over time. Laura had stayed on Long Island and built a life with her husband and kids while chasing a medical career. I had left New York behind, throwing myself into motherhood and marriage in Texas.

It was good to be home again, but I wasn't sure I felt more content here than I had in Texas.

Reality quickly overshadowed the novelty of returning home. Two months passed, and Michael still hadn't found a job. We began dipping into our savings. The four of us were crammed into a single bedroom, and it was becoming clear we couldn't stay with my parents much longer. Though my mother insisted she was fine, I could see the strain wearing on her.

I started searching for a house on the eastern side of Long Island and found a bi-level home in Hempstead listed for $50,000, which included an in-ground pool. Michael seemed interested at first, but soon came up with a dozen excuses for why we couldn't buy it.

By the end of the summer, he was offered a job in Atlanta and convinced me to move again. He promised we could buy a house there. Reluctantly, I agreed to leave New York again.

Chapter 14 | Georgia Bound

Georgia's landscape was beautiful — rolling hills, glassy lakes, and trees thick with green. But the houses were spaced farther apart, and there wasn't the same sense of community I had known in New York.

We moved into a worn-down three-bedroom rental with a fenced yard. It needed work — the walls were stained yellow, the ceilings grimy — but Michael had promised the landlord we'd paint it if he let us move in early. I should've known what that meant. Michael was always full of promises and short on follow-through.

I waited a week, then another. The brushes never came out. So, one morning, I rolled up my sleeves, bought the paint myself, and got to work. It wasn't perfect, but it felt good to do something, to take control of one small piece of our messy life. From then on, painting became my job.

Whenever I brought up buying a home of our own, Michael gave vague answers. "Soon," he'd say, and then "someday." Each time, hope flickered and died a little more. I swallowed my disappointment, afraid to spark his sarcasm or provoke the eye-rolling contempt that always made me feel small.

The anger didn't vanish—it simmered. Quietly. Constantly. Like a pressure cooker sealed tight.

Rainstorms brought new misery. The basement flooded every time, filling with foul-smelling water that took days to drain. The air turned thick with the stench of mildew and disappointment.

Jason lay in bed, his skin hot to the touch, his tiny body trembling beneath the blankets. I could hear his labored breathing from across the room. At the kitchen table, Annmarie sat quietly, her little hand gripping a crayon as she pressed it across the paper. The scratch-scratch-scratch of her coloring was the only sound in the house.

Outside, winter had trailed me to Georgia like an unwelcome shadow. Brown leaves spun from the trees, drifting down like fragile parachutes. Even though the winters here weren't as bitter, I still dreaded them. Cold meant isolation—long, empty hours inside with nothing but the static-filled hum of rabbit-ear television. I twisted the antenna, trying to get a clearer picture, but it was of no use. Staring out the window, I thought maybe cable would make the days more bearable. I picked up the phone and made the call.

A moment later, the front door creaked open. Michael stepped inside, and the children ran to him, clinging to his legs like they hadn't seen him in days.

"Jason's sick again," I said softly. "The doctor thinks it might be mold. And I think there's more water leaking into the basement."

Michael let out a long sigh, tossing his keys onto the counter. "I just walked through the door," he said sharply. "Can I have one hour—just one hour—to unwind before you hand me a list of problems? I've been dealing with people all day. I'm exhausted."

I bit down on the lump rising in my throat. "At least you get to talk to people," I murmured. "I'm stuck here with two little kids all day. I can't even remember the last time I had an actual conversation with an adult. I think I've forgotten how."

"Find a friend," he muttered. "Better yet—find a job."

"A job? Are you serious? Who's going to take care of the kids? Who's going to clean the house, cook the meals, run the errands? There's no one else here."

"Other women manage it."

"Well, I'm not like other women!" I shouted, frustration spilling out faster than I could hold it back.

He shook his head, already tired of the argument. "I had a rough day. They brought in a new manager who doesn't know Jack-shit about carpentry."

"Then talk to your boss. Stand up for yourself."

"I can't do that," he recoiled, rolling his eyes. "What would you know about any of it? You're just a housewife."

I flinched.

"Do you think this is easy?" he went on. "I bust my ass six days a week while you sit around all day."

"Sit around?" My voice rose with the heat of it. "Who do you think scrubs the toilets? Who cooks your meals, washes your dirty clothes, cleans up after the kids, and makes sure this house doesn't fall apart? I don't sit—I work just as hard as you, maybe harder!"

"Calm down," he said, holding up his hands as if I were some hysterical woman in a movie. "I didn't mean it."

Tears burned in my eyes. "I never wanted to leave Long Island again," I cried. "You promised it would be better this time, but you lied. You dragged us down here, and everything is worse!"

A few days later, I paced the living room, pretending to tidy up while I waited for Michael to leave for work. He lingered at the kitchen table, sipping his second cup of coffee like he had all the time in the world. I kept glancing nervously out the window, silently begging the cable guy not to arrive early. The air felt thick with anticipation.

Finally, Michael grabbed his keys and headed out the door without so much as a goodbye. The moment his truck pulled out of the driveway, I let out a long breath.

Ten minutes later, a knock echoed through the house.

When I opened the door, a tall man in a dark blue polo shirt and jeans stood there, adjusting his Serengeti sunglasses. "Hi, I'm Austin Braun from Satellite

Systems," he said. Our eyes met, and for a brief second, the world narrowed.

"I'm here to install your cable," he added with a smile.

"Come in," I said, stepping aside. "The wires are up in the attic."

"Upstaaares?" he repeated with a playful grin, mimicking my accent. "Where are you from?"

"New Yawk."

"I figured," he chuckled.

"You don't sound like you're from around here either."

"Kansas," he said proudly. "Born and raised. A real country boy."

I walked him to the hall and reached up to tug the attic ladder down. As I pulled it open, I caught the way his gaze lingered just a little too long. I suddenly became aware of my legs, bare beneath my shortest pair of shorts, and the thin cotton tank clinging to my skin in the humidity.

He climbed the ladder, and I found myself watching him — watching the way his broad back shifted beneath the damp fabric of his shirt, the way his sun-streaked hair curled slightly at the collar.

He was up there a while. I heard the soft thud of tools and the occasional curse under his breath. Once, he came down to get something from his truck, then disappeared back into the attic.

Eventually, the ladder creaked again, and he climbed down, the attic door snapping shut behind him. His shirt clung to his back, soaked with sweat, and beads of moisture glistened along his forehead.

"Whew," he said, wiping his brow. "Feels like a furnace up there."

"You want something cold? I've got iced tea."

"I'd love some," he said. "Could probably drink a gallon."

"It's unsweetened," I warned. "Not like the syrup they serve down here. I can add sugar if you want."

"Nah, this is perfect." He drained the glass in one long gulp. I poured him another without thinking, almost grateful for something to do with my hands.

"So," he said casually, "Georgia's a long way from New York. What brought you down here?"

I paused, turning back to the sink. "It's a long story," I said, rinsing his glass. "Let's just say life took a few unexpected turns."

He didn't press. Just nodded, then packed up his tools and snapped his toolbox shut.

"If anything goes wrong, give me a call," he said, handing me a card. "Welcome to Georgia, city girl. Don't let 'em change you."

I laughed, though something about the way he said it made my smile falter. It wasn't just a joke—it was a warning. A reminder.

"I won't," I said quietly.

Chapter 15 | Pillar of Salt

My mother had hinted at trouble when I was in New York — quiet, careful mentions that things weren't right between her and my father. But I never imagined it would come to this. After twenty-five years and four children, their marriage had unraveled.

I sat by the phone that morning, heart pounding, willing it to ring. When it finally did, I snatched it up.

"Have you heard from Dad?" I asked, my voice tight.

"No," she said quietly. "He just... packed up and left."

There was a hollow pause, the kind that settles between two people when words feel too small.

"What are you going to do?" I finally whispered.

"I don't know," she said. "But learn from my mistakes, Florence. Don't ever put yourself in a position where you have to rely on a man to take care of you."

Her voice was steady, but I heard the heartbreak beneath it.

I'd always believed my father would be there—emotionally absent, but his presence unquestioned.

"Maybe he'll come to his senses," I said.

"I don't think so." She sighed. "I'll call you later."

As I sat in the dining room, nursing my fifth cup of coffee, her words echoed in my head, louder than I wanted to admit. Michael had recently dismissed me as "just a housewife," and until that moment, I hadn't let myself consider the danger in giving everything to a life that could walk out the door without warning. Now I was forced to. Our childhood house was being listed. It would soon belong to strangers. I couldn't go back—even if I wanted to.

Annmarie and Jason were eating their breakfast cereal. I stared out the window, feeling lonely and adrift. The phone rang again, shaking me out of my gloom.

"Hi, Florence."

"Yes, who's this?" The voice sounded familiar.

"It's Austin. Don't you remember me?"

"Oh—right! You're the Kansas boy who hooked up my cable."

"I've been thinking about you," he said. "I miss hearing your New York accent."

"Really?" I'd nearly forgotten about him.

As we talked, Jason started riding his tricycle through the living room, and Annmarie sat mesmerized by the television. I knew I should hang up—but I didn't. Instead, I twirled a strand of hair around my finger, a nervous habit I'd had since I was a child. "You know I'm married, right?"

"There's no harm in talking, is there?"

"I guess not," I murmured.

We talked for over an hour. It was the most pleasant morning I'd had in a long time.

"Can I call you again?" he asked.

"I suppose so."

"Good. I could listen to you talk for hours."

I laughed. "I could talk for hours."

Almost every morning, Austin called. Our daily conversations felt harmless — just friendly voices on the other end of the line. I told myself I wasn't doing anything wrong.

"We should meet for lunch," he suggested one day.

"I wish I could, but..."

"Oh, come on. I promise not to bite."

Jason and Annmarie were sprawled on the floor, playing with their toys, only a few feet away, completely unaware of my conversation.

"It's not that. I have kids."

"Don't you have a sitter?"

"No, I don't know anyone here."

"What about daycare?"

"They've never been."

"I'm going to keep asking," he said with a laugh. "Find someone."

"I'll try — but I can't promise anything."

After we hung up, I remembered a billboard I'd seen: *Hourly Walk-in Daycare — Seven Days a Week*. It was only two blocks away.

"Get your shoes on, kids," I said. "We're going out for a little while."

"Where are we going, Mommy?" Jason asked.

"We're going to check out a fun place to play."

"Are there other kids?" Annmarie asked.

"Yes. Lots of them."

We pulled into the parking lot, and it was nearly full — a good sign.

Inside, the owner greeted me warmly while the kids dashed off toward the play area. After a quick tour, I was both impressed and reassured. *I have a babysitter.*

The next time Austin called, I agreed to meet him for lunch. I dropped the children off at the daycare center. The cheerful sound of children playing eased my guilt slightly. I knew what I was doing was wrong, but the thrill of the unknown made my hands tremble on the wheel. As I got closer to the restaurant, my nerves began to fray.

Austin wasn't there yet, but the hostess led me to a booth. I still had time to back out, to call the whole thing off. But I didn't. I stayed.

He appeared, walking toward the table. Dressed in jeans and a button-down shirt, he looked rugged, like a cowboy. The softness in his eyes disarmed me. My stomach fluttered as he slid into the booth across from me.

"I'm glad you agreed to meet me," he said. "You're so beautiful, I can't believe you're really here."

I hadn't heard words like that in a long time, and I soaked in the warmth of his admiration.

The server arrived with two glasses of water.

"Can I take your order?"

"I'll have a burger platter and a Coke," Austin said.

"I'll have the same," I said.

She walked away, and we continued our conversation.

"What made you leave Kansas?" I asked.

"It was time. Satellite TV was booming, and the cable company needed someone to travel. Since I was unattached, why not?"

"What's it like there?"

"Small town. A lot like this, just flatter," he said.

"I don't like small towns."

"Maybe I can change your mind," he said, holding my gaze.

I was glad I came. The food arrived, but neither of us wanted to break the moment.

"Is there anything else I can get you?" the server asked.

"No," we said in unison, eager for her to leave.

"Are you Italian?" Austin asked.

"Yes. How did you know?"

"Those big brown eyes," he teased.

We lingered, talking and laughing for over an hour. His eyes rarely left mine.

I only glanced away to check the time. "I should go."

"Already?"

"I promised my kids that I wouldn't be long."

"I get it," he said. "But promise me we'll have lunch again." He put a twenty-dollar bill under the salt and pepper shakers, and we walked outside. I scanned the parking lot, relieved I didn't see anyone I knew.

As I opened the car door, Austin stepped closer, gently pulling me toward him. Our bodies met, and we kissed — warm, soft, electric.

"Follow me back to my apartment," he whispered, his voice low and urgent.

I hesitated. "No, I'd better not."

"Why?"

"I need to pick up my children."

"They're probably having fun. Can't you leave them just a little longer?"

His charm was impossible to resist.

"I guess I can." In my heart, I knew if I were alone with Austin, the temptation would be too much to resist, but I wasn't ready to go home — not yet.

We both got into our cars. I waited for him to pull out of the parking spot and followed behind. Feeling like a teenager cutting school, a flush of excitement coursed through me. I thought of my mother — how she had been faithful her entire life. And look where it got her.

A few minutes later, we arrived at his apartment complex. He punched in a code, and the gate slowly opened. I pulled into the parking spot beside him.

He opened the front door. The place was quiet, but the air held the unmistakable scent of testosterone.

"Do you live alone?" I asked.

"No. I've got a few roommates, but they're at work."

"How many?"

"There were four. One moved out and went back home." Austin sat on the couch and patted the cushion next to him. "Come sit."

I hesitated but sat down and grabbed a throw pillow, hugging it to my lap like a shield. *I shouldn't be here*, I thought.

As if reading my mind, Austin gently pulled me toward him and kissed me, slowly and sweetly.

"Come on," he whispered and took my hand. He led me through the hallway into his bedroom. It was still daylight, but he lit a candle on the nightstand. Then he unbuttoned his shirt and tossed it over the back of a chair.

"I want you so much," he said.

"Do you have protection?" I asked.

"No, but we can be careful."

I froze. "I want you too… but I can't get pregnant. Maybe we shouldn't."

"I understand," he said, reaching for his shirt.

"Wait," I said, stopping him. Something inside me still yearned for him. I craved closeness—and being wanted.

He turned and kissed me again. His hands roamed across my back, then down. With a shiver of anticipation, I let go. Like falling into a dream, everything slowed.

He began to unbutton my blouse. I didn't stop him. As he undressed me, the cool air kissed my bare skin—or maybe it was the thrill of surrender.

He kicked off his shoes, unbuckled his belt, and slid out of his jeans.

I shouldn't be here, I thought, but the moment had already taken me. Austin pulled me into him, and all resistance vanished.

As the sun dipped lower in the sky, it cast soft shadows across the bedroom walls.

"I have to go," I said, jumping out of bed.

Austin reluctantly got dressed and walked me to my car."Can I see you tomorrow?"

"We'll see," I said, letting him kiss me one more time.

I started the engine and rolled down the window. He watched me drive off. The moment he disappeared from my rearview mirror, I hit the gas, suddenly anxious. The kids had been at daycare for hours. What if they were wondering where I was?

I had fifty dollars in my purse—just enough to cover the daycare fee. My checkbook was also in my bag, but I preferred not to use it. Michael rarely checked the register, but there was always a chance.

I felt another wave of guilt as I walked into the daycare center, but before I could dwell on it, the children ran up to me, arms open.

"Can we stay longer?" Annmarie asked.

"No, we have to get home," I said, brushing her hair back. "Maybe we'll come again tomorrow."

"Yay!" she squealed, bouncing with excitement.

Jason, however, didn't share her enthusiasm.

"What's wrong?" I asked.

"There was a boy who kept pinching me. I don't want to come back."

"Next time, pinch him back," I said, even though I knew he never would—and it wasn't the right response.

Driving home, my thoughts drifted to Austin. I was so distracted, I barely realized I'd turned onto our street. Trees blocked the view until I was nearly at the house.

My heart thumped. Michael's truck was in the driveway. Panic stirred in my gut. I wasn't sure that I could hide my guilty conscience. I ushered the children out of the car and into the house, trying to appear calm as I went straight to the kitchen to start dinner.

"Where were you?" Michael asked.

I felt my face flush. "Shopping—you know, the usual."

"We were at daycare," Jason said.

Michael raised an eyebrow. "Daycare? Why?"

"I thought it might be fun for them to be around other kids," I said, keeping my tone light. "They need that kind of interaction."

He studied my face, skeptical. But after a beat, he nodded. For now, he seemed satisfied.

Chapter 16 | Truth or Dare

Just thinking about Austin made me smile. He filled the empty hours of my day and made me feel wanted — loved. I knew the affair was reckless, but I couldn't stay away from him.

Needing to confide in someone, I turned to my sister-in-law. Kelly was always cheerful, and while she never said anything outright, I suspected she was having an affair of her own. I felt guilty hiding Kelly's secret from my brother, but I was doing the same thing. Who was I to judge?

When I told her about Austin, she burst out laughing. "You? Having an affair? I don't believe it."

After that, she called me every day for updates. It felt good to have someone to talk to, and I didn't see a reason to doubt her loyalty.

Every weekday, I dropped the kids at daycare, drove to Austin's apartment, and stepped into a world where nothing else existed. I joined the gym and sometimes left Michael to watch the kids after dinner.

Inside Austin's apartment, we'd head straight to his bedroom and lock the door. His roommates' voices — beer bottles clinking, sports on the TV — faded as the music played on the stereo. The world outside disappeared. There was only Austin and me.

But the deeper I fell, the harder it became to leave. I stopped thinking about what came next — because there *was* no next — just stolen moments.

"I wish you could stay the night," Austin said one evening.

"Me too," I whispered. "But what would I tell Michael?"

"I don't know. Make something up," he said, tugging me back into bed.

"I have to leave. I don't have a choice."

"You do," he said quietly. "Leave him. Move in with me."

"I can't," I said, laughing nervously. "I have two kids."

The look on his face changed. I saw the disappointment in his eyes. He didn't say anything, but I could feel everything he held back.

I told myself I loved him, but I had never really considered leaving my marriage — or my children. If I truly loved him, wouldn't I want to be with him for real, not just behind a locked door?

And that's when it hit me — the affair had gone too far.

Driving home that night, each mile brought me closer to what *did* matter. I couldn't wait to see my children, to hear them laugh.

When I pulled into the driveway, the house was dark except for the flickering light of the TV. Michael was in the living room. I figured the kids were already in bed, so I sat in the car for a moment.

Inside, Michael looked up.

"What's wrong?"

"Kelly called," he said. "She wanted to know where you were."

"Kelly?" I repeated, heart pounding. She knew exactly where I was.

"I told her you were at the gym. That's where you were, right?"

"Yes, of course."

The next day, Michael didn't return from work. I stared at the phone. He hadn't called. That wasn't like him. He always let me know if he was going to be late. As the sun dipped below the horizon, a cold front rolled through Georgia. The wind howled outside, rattling the windows and my nerves. Still, no sign of him.

Not knowing who else to turn to, I called my brother.

"Have you heard from Michael today?" I asked.

"No," he said. "What's going on?"

"He never came home. I'm getting worried."

"Well, I haven't seen him, sis."

"Okay," I said, trying to sound calm. "If you do hear from him, please let me know."

After putting the kids to bed, I turned on the television to distract myself. A red alert flashed across the screen—**BREAKING NEWS: Ice Storm Warning.** Footage rolled of jackknifed trucks and cars spinning across frozen highways. The roads were a mess. Panic twisted my nerves.

Maybe he'd been in an accident. Maybe he was hurt. The guilt hit me like a punch—I deserved this. I was being punished. What if the last thing he remembered was a lie I told?

The phone rang.

"Hi, Florence." My mother's voice came through, soft but anxious. "I just saw the news. That storm looks awful. Are you okay?"

"Michael hasn't come home. I'm worried something's happened."

"Maybe he just can't get to a phone, honey."

"No… I don't know. Something feels wrong."

She tried to comfort me, but I could hear the worry in her silence. "Get some sleep. I'll call you in the morning."

After we hung up, I called the hospital. The line was busy. Again and again, all I got was a buzz or an endless busy signal.

I curled up on the couch, unable to sleep. *If something happened to Michael, I'll never forgive myself.*

Staring at the ceiling, I listened for the hum of his car in the driveway. Nothing.

At sunrise, I called the hospital again. Finally, someone answered.

"Was Michael Corrigan admitted last night?"

The receptionist paused to check. "No, ma'am. No one by that name was admitted."

Relief rushed through me—he wasn't hurt. But if he was okay, then *where was he?*

I called my brother again. This time, Kelly picked up.

"Have you heard from Michael?" I asked quickly.

Silence.

"Kelly? Have you *seen* him?"

"Yes," she said slowly. "He's right here."

"What?"

"He's been here all night."

"But I called. Frank said he didn't know where he was."

Kelly gave a little laugh. "Well… Michael didn't want us to tell you."

"What? Why? What's going on? Put him on the phone."

"He doesn't want to talk to you."

"Why?" I whispered.

After a pause, Kelly's voice, teasing and smug, said… "You *know* why… You're busted!"

Chapter 17 | Fallout

After a fitful night, I awoke to the sound of Jason and Annmarie playing with their toys, oblivious to the storm outside.

Shortly before noon, Annmarie ran to the window. "Daddy's home!" she squealed.

Jason ran to join her. "Daddy, Daddy!"

Michael walked in. The kids ran to him and clung to his legs, but his somber face sent them back to their toys.

Without a word, he went to the bedroom. I stood in the doorway. His face was blank.

"I didn't mean for it to happen. I was depressed and —"

He stared at me, his expression dark and ominous.

"Aren't you going to talk to me?"

"You told me that you were going to the gym. I can't believe this. I've been babysitting every night while you were off with someone else."

"I'm sorry," I said. "I know what I did was wrong. I was confused."

"I need time to think," he said, pulling a tattered suitcase from under the bed and stuffing it with clothes.

"I didn't mean for it to turn out like this," I said softly.

He looked up, eyes blazing. "How *did* you mean for it to turn out?"

"It was a mistake. You're always working, and I was lonely. I'm not happy."

"Maybe your boyfriend can make you happy," he snapped, slamming the suitcase shut. "Go cry to him."

"That's not fair. I've been telling you I've been depressed for months. You never listen."

"What do you expect me to do?"

"That's the problem. You don't care. Maybe if you let me vent, I wouldn't have felt so alone."

"You're never happy."

I opened my mouth to respond, but nothing came out. *Maybe he's right. Maybe nothing will ever make me happy.*

"What about the children?"

"You should've thought about them *before*." He turned to me at the door. "Oh—and I canceled the credit cards."

As the door slammed, my heart clenched. He was gone.

It had never occurred to me—how would I survive without him? Two children. No job. No education. Far from my family. I was alone.

My eyes looked like two raisins stuck in a puffy batch of cookie dough. After crying nonstop, I had an empty hole in my stomach. Where would I go? What would I do?

I could hear the children playing, oblivious to how their lives might change. I went into the bathroom to wash my tear-stained face.

At the sound of Michael's truck, the children ran to the door.

"We missed you, Daddy," they chimed.

"I missed you, too," he said and hugged them.

"Can we talk?" I begged. "I know you're angry. I don't blame you, but I need help until I find a job and someone to help watch the children while I'm at work."

"Are you still seeing him?"

"No. I broke it off," I said, even though I hadn't told Austin yet. "I was lonely, Michael. He was there. You weren't."

His face softened. "Maybe it's my fault you were lonely. I don't want a divorce. I want to fix our marriage. I'll work less and spend more time with you and the kids."

Tears streamed down my face.

"We're a family," he said. "Let's do it for the kids."

I nodded. "Yes. I'm willing to give us another chance if you are, but we can't stay here. There's a mold problem, and it's making our children sick."

"We'll look for a house," Michael said, and hugged me.

Torn between the fantasy I'd lived in and the promise of a house, I had to forget Austin Braun.

Searching for a house, I checked real estate listings to find something we could afford. The $10,000 from our Houston, Texas house sale barely scratched the surface of what we needed.

"Maybe we can buy land and get a loan to build," I suggested.

"The cost of property is too high in this area. We would have to buy land outside of town."

"I like being close to stores and people... but I guess I can compromise if it means owning a house."

I looked through the designs in my House Beautiful magazine. One caught my eye—a bi-level plan with Swiss chalet windows. The lower level had a den that opened into the garage. The middle floor featured a sunken living room with a stone fireplace, a dining room with glass doors opening to the backyard, and a kitchen with windows overlooking the garden. Upstairs were four bedrooms and two baths—one in the master, the other in the hall. But the best part was the windows. Diamond-paneled grills with shutters. I loved the detail.

The blueprints for the home cost $100. I filled out the form and wrote out a check. Then I cut the photo from the magazine and stuck it in my purse.

I scoured the classifieds for private land sales. There were plenty of listings, but most were for multiple acres—too much for us. Eventually, I convinced Michael to let me call a real estate agent.

"We only have one small lot," the agent said. "But it's by the lake."

"By the lake? That sounds great!"

We jumped in his car and drove about twenty miles north, past Fort Klamath. The lot was near Diamond Lake, with the water glinting through the trees.

"It's steep," I said, eyeing the slope.

"Most land out here is, but an excavating crew can handle that," he assured me.

"What about electricity, water, sewage?"

"You'd need to apply through the county."

"Can we add a contingency?"

"A what?"

"A clause in the contract to get our deposit back if we can't get permits," I said, proud of myself.

"I guess we can include that."

Good thing we did. The water table was too high for a sewage system, and the deal fell through.

I went back to the classifieds with a new focus— Fort Klamath. I found another listing, not on the lake, but on a cul-de-sac.

"I found some land," I told Michael when he came home. "It's out in the country."

"Great," he said. "We'll check it out this weekend."

"No, we need to see it now."

He groaned. "I just worked all day."

"It's only thirty minutes north."

He finally agreed, and I hustled the kids into the car before he could change his mind.

As we drove, the countryside unfolded like a quilt of golden fields and emerald copses. The air had that crisp, earthy smell of late summer, and I rolled down the window to let it in. "I think it's down this road," I said, my voice tinged with anticipation.

We turned left onto a narrow lane, where towering trees arched overhead. Their leaves whispered secrets to the wind, forming a dappled pattern of light and shadow on the gravel beneath us. Michael's eyes lit up—this was his kind of place, secluded and wild, like something plucked from his dreams.

At the end of the lane, a rough clearing opened up, edged with tangled underbrush and tall grass that swayed lazily in the breeze. A steep, rutted dirt path climbed into the trees, beckoning us with the promise of discovery. Michael didn't wait—he was out of the car in an instant, his boots crunching over twigs and dry leaves, leaving me to wrangle the kids from their car seats.

"Wait up!" I called, hurrying after him. The brush tugged at my jeans as I followed his eager strides.

When I caught up, he stood in the middle of the clearing, turning slowly, his face alive with excitement.

"Where's the blueprint?" he asked, glancing back at me as the last light of day spilled through the canopy above.

"In the car!" I said, dashing back to retrieve it. The paper felt cool and crisp in my hands as I handed it to him. He held it up to the fading sunlight, squinting as he pieced together its promise with the land around us.

"It's perfect," he said, his voice a mix of awe and certainty. "I think we found our land!"

Chapter 18 | Sweat Equity

After signing the paperwork, the land was officially ours. All we needed now was a construction loan. Confident that the bank would approve us, I completed the application and submitted it.

A week passed. Not a word. Growing anxious, I called and asked to speak with the loan officer.

"I was just about to call you," he said.

I let out a nervous laugh. "I was starting to think you forgot about us. We're excited to get started —"

"I'm sorry," he said, cutting me off.

My fingers tightened around the phone. "Sorry?"

"Your loan was denied."

"Denied? Why?"

"You haven't lived in Georgia long enough to be considered established."

"But we bank with you. We're good customers."

"I wish I could do something," he said gently. "If it were up to me, I'd approve it. But I don't make the rules."

"Fine," I said with a hint of annoyance. "I'll find another bank."

"Best of luck to you, ma'am."

The dream suddenly felt like it was slipping away.

I hung up and drove to another bank. The kids rushed off to a play area while I filled out a new application. Moments later, a man stepped out of his office and extended his hand.

"Jim Buckley," he said. "Nice to meet you."

I followed him inside, chattering nervously about moving our accounts to this bank.

"Have a seat," he said, scanning my paperwork.

I sank into the plush chair and watched his smile fade as he read.

"We own the land," I added quickly. "That has to count for something." I stood to leave. "You were my last hope."

"Exactly what does your husband do for a living?" he asked.

"He's in the carpenters' union."

Mr. Buckley's eyes lit up. "Have you ever heard of sweat equity?"

"No," I said.

"Well, it's not conventional," he said, "but if your husband can do most of the labor—framing, drywall, painting—well, that work has real value. That value can be applied toward your equity."

"Really?" I said, hope flickering again.

He nodded. "I want to help you, Florence. I'll need a list of everything your husband can do himself. He handed me a checklist of construction stages, each with an estimated dollar value.

I left the bank feeling like I accomplished something.

That night at the dinner table, I made the announcement.

"The bank approved the loan. But there's a catch — we have to build the house ourselves."

"Ourselves?" Michael raised a brow. "That's a lot of work."

"It's the only way," I said. "We can do it."

He thought it over. "If I'm going to be the contractor, maybe I should quit my job. We'll have enough money to live on during the build."

I hesitated. It felt risky. But when he pointed out how much faster we could finish, I gave in.

Michael wielded the chainsaw with a steady hand, its grating roar splitting the forest's quiet. Each tree he felled left behind a bittersweet scent of fresh pine and damp bark, mingling with the earthy musk of overturned soil. His jaw tightened with every cut, as if he were excising something deeper than roots from the land.

Nearby, I heaped branches and snapped twigs into the fire pit, the dry crackle of flames meeting green wood filling the air. My muscles burned, my palms stung with the sting of raw blisters, but I pressed on, fueled by a stubborn tenacity. Smoke curled upward, carrying the sharp, acrid perfume of burning sap and leaves.

Chapter 19 | Moving Day

The land was muddy, the driveway slope unyielding. Trucks couldn't make it up the hill, so every delivery was dumped at the bottom—lumber, cement blocks, stacks of drywall. And that meant hauling it all up the driveway by hand. One board at a time, I trudged up the hill, soaked and aching. But I didn't care. This was my dream house, and I was going to help build it, no matter how long it took or how hard it got. I wore a necklace of dirt instead of pearls. My hands were rough with splinters and grit, my nails perpetually in ruins.

After each phase, inspectors signed off, and the bank released another round of funds. Slowly, the house began to take shape.

Sheltered from the winds that had stripped the leaves from the trees, I wandered through the interior, basking in the sunlight pouring through our newly installed windows. I paused in the dining room, admiring the decorative diamond grills. The light danced through the panes just the way I'd imagined. I had wanted them throughout the house, but we didn't have enough money.

Outside, the trees had begun to bud, tiny green leaves promising spring. I was busy sealing grout on the floor tiles when I heard Michael calling my name. I wiped my hands and stepped outside, taking a moment to admire the oak entry door I'd found on clearance. It had etched glass, with two delicate bluebirds encircled by frosted vines. It was a steal, and my favorite find.

Michael was slumped at the edge of the driveway, his head in his hands.

"It's gone," he said.

"What's gone?"

"The money for the bathroom fixtures... The plumber ran off with it."

"What? Are you sure?"

I saw the stress in his face. "We'll figure something out," I said. "Maybe we can do the landscaping ourselves."

"That'll help," he agreed. "I was going to hire someone to pave the driveway... but we'll have to do that, too."

The concrete truck backed into position at the bottom of the driveway, its chute angled just right. As the wet mix poured down, Michael worked quickly, smoothing it with practiced strokes.

When the truck pulled away, we stood at the bottom of the slope, both admiring the fresh pour. That's when we noticed the clouds—thick, gray, and moving fast.

"I think it's going to rain," I said.

"Quick!" Michael snapped. "Run to the store and get some plastic sheeting. If it rains, we'll lose it!"

I hesitated, staring at the sky, stunned by how fast it had darkened.

"Now!" he shouted. "I'll watch the kids."

I jumped in the car and sped toward Home Depot, heart pounding. The build wasn't going as I'd imagined. The stress and delays were taking a toll on me.

By the time I reached the store, a light drizzle had already begun. Inside, I darted down aisles, unsure where to look. In a moment of panic, I asked a fellow customer for help. Thankfully, he knew exactly where to go and led me straight to the plastic sheeting.

The wind was howling by the time I reached the checkout. As I crossed the parking lot, small stones pelted me, whipped up by gusts. Then came the downpour, fast and merciless. I was soaked before I could unlock the door.

On the way home, rain slammed against the windshield in sheets. The wipers worked furiously but couldn't keep up. I hit a puddle, and water splashed up so high it blinded me for a moment. I gripped the wheel and squinted at the red blur of taillights ahead, praying I was still in my lane.

When I finally turned down our road, the storm had already moved on. The rain had slowed to a whisper. Sunlight broke through the clouds. I floored it toward the cul-de-sac, clinging to one last shred of hope.

Maybe it hadn't rained here.

Michael stood at the bottom of the driveway, arms slack at his sides. He didn't move toward the car.

I stepped out slowly.

The driveway was ruined. Rivulets of water carved jagged lines through the concrete. Furrows, pits, erosion. All of Michael's hard work was washed away.

The loss hit hard, tightening our already strained budget. We pressed forward—hammering, sanding, spackling, and painting.

By August, the sun blazed like a perfect ball of fire overhead. Our lease was almost up. If we didn't finish soon, we'd have to renew.

"We could move in now," Michael said. "Save money on rent."

"But the house isn't finished. We don't even have appliances."

"We could barbecue," he said. "Keep food in a cooler. It'll be like camping!"

The kids squealed with delight at the idea.

I hesitated. The warmth of their excitement tugged at me.

"Yeah," Michael added, suddenly optimistic. "We'll bring our beds."

I wanted to live there so badly, despite the missing kitchen appliances and the fact that half the walls still needed painting. Underneath it all, I had a nagging feeling. *What if Michael lost the motivation to finish the house?*

With a mix of reluctance and exhilaration, I agreed. We were moving into our own home, one we had built with our own hands.

Michael rented a U-Haul, and I drove to the supermarket for boxes. We spent the next two days packing up our lives into cardboard boxes. The house was bare by that afternoon—just walls, echoes, and mold. As I stood in the empty living room, I whispered to myself, *No more landlords. No more leases. This is it.*

The kids were giddy, racing from room to room. Jason ran upstairs ahead of us as we carried up the last load of furniture.

"Can I have my bed by the window?" he shouted.

"Of course," I said, setting down a box. "But go play while we finish."

"I don't have anyone to play with."

"Where's Annmarie?"

"She's with the girl down the street. Her name's Lilly."

I smiled. "Perfect. She'll have a best friend to grow up with."

As I predicted, Michael stopped working on the house when we moved in. I was disheartened at the construction debris still piled up in the driveway. Supplies were strewn everywhere. I wanted to complain, but I knew I'd be accused of nagging. Instead, I quietly walked around, picking up nails and screws, afraid one would end up in a tire — or worse, in the bottom of one of my children's feet.

Chapter 20 | Kept Women

Georgia didn't seem so bad. There were plenty of trees, and the small town had little traffic.

Every morning, I packed the children's school lunches, slipped in a cute little note and a special treat, and added their sandwiches.

We walked to the corner to wait for the bus. Two other mothers were standing at the bus stop with their children. I still hadn't met my neighbors, so it seemed like the perfect opportunity to get acquainted. They seemed to know each other very well. Busy chatting, they didn't notice us at first.

As we approached, the conversation came to a halt. They both gaped at me. It made me feel uneasy, but I managed a smile. Annmarie ran ahead to join her new friend, Lily, who was standing alongside her mother.

"Hi, I'm Ellen, Lily's mom."

"Oh yes. Annmarie told me all about her. I'm glad they're friends."

"I'm Tami," the other woman said. "Welcome to the neighborhood."

"Thank you."

"How do you like it here in Georgia?" Ellen asked.

"So far, I like it."

"Do you work?" Tami asked.

"No, I'm a stay-at-home mom."

"Oh."

I could feel her disdain. Thank goodness the school bus lumbered down the street and flashed its red lights. I kissed my children goodbye, and they scrambled onto the bus, leaving me alone with the mothers.

"Well, I have to go to work," Ellen said. "I don't want to be late."

"Me, too," Tami added.

As I turned to leave, I heard Ellen whisper. "Another Yankee! Actually, a Damn Yankee. I don't think she's leaving."

Tami Laughed. "I wonder how she walks in those heels."

I looked down at my feet and realized my shoes were out of place in the country. The weight of displacement pressed into my core. I was out of sync with the slow-paced rhythm of the South.

Reluctantly, I put away my heels. Sneakers, jeans, and T-shirts became my new attire. They were more appropriate for country living and practical for working in the garden, which had become my favorite pastime. I was content to dig in the dirt, but I found it challenging to plant flowers and shrubbery, which I moved from one spot to another, trying to find the best sunlight. Working in my garden was an easy way to escape reality. Nothing else existed. Dogwood flowers bloomed in white, and Redbud trees flowered in the woods. I planted Hibiscus flowers that bloomed in red, white, and peach, and the forsythia was vibrant with yellow buds.

Within the safety of my marriage, my confidence soared. Able to leap tall buildings in a single bound, I became "Supermom." I enrolled Annmarie in ballet class. Even though my daughter was shy and didn't keep up with the other little girls, I thought she looked cute in her little pink tutu and ballet shoes. Jason was still too young for an activity, but I thought he might do well in Cub Scouts.

The scent of brown sugar or chocolate filled the house every day before the children returned from school. We had a ritual. First, they ate their snacks and told me about their day at school. Then I would help them with their homework. The hiss of the air brakes from the bus down the street shook me out of my daydreams. I rushed to take the cookies out of the oven.

Annmarie burst through the front door first. "We're home!" she announced.

"I smell cookies!" Jason shouted. He threw off his backpack and scrambled up on the kitchen stool.

I poured each of them a glass of milk. "What's wrong, Annmarie? You look upset."

"Nothing!"

"What's a kept woman?" Jason asked with genuine curiosity.

"Where'd you hear that?"

"Lily's mom says you're a kept woman," Jason murmured with a hint of shame.

I frowned. "Why does Lily say that?"

"Because you don't work," Annmarie said.

"I do work. I work here at home, taking care of you and your brother."

"But you don't have a real job, like Lily's mom."

"Lily isn't home right now, is she?"

"No, she goes to the after-school program."

"Is that where you'd like to go after school?"

"No," Jason cried. "I want to come home."

"What else does Lily's mom say?"

"She says you're not dependent," Jason said.

"Do you mean independent?"

"Uh-huh. Yeah. What's that?"

"Independent is not relying on someone else to care for you."

"Do you rely on Daddy?" he asked.

"Yeah, I guess so." I felt small in his eyes. I stretched a piece of Saran Wrap over the remaining cookies.

"Why don't you both go out and play? We'll do your homework later."

Kept woman! The comment struck a nerve.

Increasingly, women were leaving their aprons behind to join the workforce. They had no tolerance for women like me.

Feeling down, I called my mother and told her what had happened.

"If it bothers you, maybe you should find a part-time job while the children are at school."

"What kind of job could I get? I never went to college."

"They're always looking for substitute teachers. Maybe you can get a job at the school."

"That's a great idea, Mom. They're building a new elementary school. It's due to open next fall. I'm sure they'll be hiring. It would get me out of the house, and I'd be home in time for the children."

I hung up and called the board of education to apply for a position.

Chapter 21 | J-E-L-L-O

The summer flew by, but still, there was no news from the school board. I was about to give up when I received a letter. My hands trembled as I tore open the envelope.

"We regret to inform you that, at this time, we do not have any open positions for substitute teaching. We do have an opening in the cafeteria, however, if you are interested. Please call to schedule an interview."

I crushed the letter and tossed it in the trash. Then called my mother.

"I didn't get the job, Mom. I guess I wasn't qualified. They offered me a position in the cafeteria."

"Why don't you take it?"

"I don't want to work in a cafeteria."

"Florence, get your foot in the door. Once you're in, maybe you can ask for a transfer."

I accepted the job.

The lunchroom supervisor was a no-nonsense Southern woman I judged to be in her late fifties. She allowed no informality and insisted I call her Mrs. Waldron.

"We have stringent rules here," she said. "Everyone has to wear a hairnet on the line."

Ugh, a hairnet. How degrading, I thought, as I tucked my hair under the black web.

"This is not a fashion show," she said as if reading my mind. "Do you have a problem with that?"

"No, ma'am."

Did I just say, ma'am? It sounded so southern.

Mrs. Waldron stood up. "Come with me, and I'll show you the kitchen."

We entered the back of the cafeteria. The heat from the ovens was overwhelming, and the smell of meatloaf made my stomach turn. Mrs. Waldron handed me a scouring pad and told me to scrub the pots.

Steam billowed from the noisy dishwasher, and racks of dishes came through on a conveyor belt. It made me feel like I was in a sauna. I thought I might pass out. It wasn't what I had envisioned when I applied for a job at the school, but I needed the flexibility so I could be home with my children.

"Florence, I need you at the Jell-O station," Mrs. Waldron said. "Put on an apron."

Glad to escape the pots, I put on a white apron and tied it around my waist. The cafeteria came alive with a never-ending parade of laughing children.

Some lined up for a hot lunch, and others immediately sat at their assigned tables with brown bags from home. Both my children brown-bagged their lunches. They preferred food from home, primarily because of the surprise I always packed for them.

As the third graders filed in, a sea of bobbing heads, I searched for Jason and waved as he joined his friends at a table. The rest of the children lined up to enter the lunch line. I smiled as they handed me their trays.

"Look! It's Annmarie's mom," a boy on the line shouted.

I recognized the kids from Annmarie's class, but the line moved so quickly that I couldn't stop working to look for my daughter in the lunchroom. I did my best to keep up with the task. A bead of sweat escaped my hairnet, and red Jell-O ran down my apron.

Suddenly, I spotted my two familiar women making their way along the line. It was Tami and Ellen, my neighbors. They were dressed impeccably in skirt suits, their makeup perfect, and every hair in place.

Under the harsh cafeteria lights, my face turned as red as the Jell-O that ran down my apron. I wanted to sink under the counter.

"Hi, Florence," Ellen said in her sing-song voice.

"What are you doing here?" I asked, forcing a smile.

"We started working today as substitute teachers," Tami said.

"Substitute teachers?"

"Yes, Ellen's husband went to school with the commissioner on the school board and was able to pull a few strings to get us hired."

A twinge of resentment mingled with my embarrassment. The line kept moving but seemed to go on forever. When the last class came through, I cleaned my station and returned to scrubbing more pots, hoping no one noticed the tears that mixed with the steam of the hot water. My self-esteem fell to an all-time low. Mrs. Waldron's stern face seared into me like a hot iron.

"Did I do something wrong?"

"No. You did great at the serving line. I saw the two women who came through. By the look on your face, I take it they're not friends."

"No, not really. Those women are my neighbors. I just don't fit in."

"Gibberish," she said, eyes darkening. "Those bitches are jealous. They see you as a threat."

"A threat?"

"Of course. You're in the South, darlin' — not exactly the place for high fashion or any of that intellectual stuff. Here you are, a city girl moving into their territory. They want to prove they're as good as you."

"But I'm not like that. I didn't even finish college."

She shook her head at my naiveté.

"Unfortunately, women can be very judgmental. They mistake your kindness for weakness."

I thought I spotted a slight smile on Mrs. Waldron's lips.

"You seem like a good girl, Florence. Don't let people push you around."

I only lasted one day as a cafeteria lady. After scrubbing the last pot, I put my apron in the laundry pile and gave Mrs. Waldron my notice.

Driven by a desire to carve out my identity, I decided to return to school. I remembered an accounting teacher from my high school days. He had given me an A and told me I had a talent for recordkeeping. *Maybe I should go to college.* I straightened my posture and drove to the small community college in town, where I signed up for Accounting 101.

Chapter 22 | Above Average

At thirty-four, I still saw myself as a young woman, just one who hadn't quite figured things out. After receiving an A in my first class, I signed up for Accounting 102. I was technically a part-time student, but even that felt like a lot. I knew I wouldn't graduate for years, but somehow, that didn't bother me.

I thought accounting might be a good fit, but I considered nursing — until I remembered how much science and formulas intimidated me.

I found my major by accident. Ever since I was a girl, I'd wanted to learn French. When it came time to fulfill the language requirement, I signed up. The teacher, a stylish blonde in crisp white pants and black heels, had emigrated from France after marrying an American soldier. Along with the language, she shared fascinating stories about French history and culture. Her passion was infectious. I was hooked. That's when I declared my major in International Studies.

The coursework on European culture intrigued me, but learning a new language proved challenging. With my thick Brooklyn accent, I butchered the pronunciation. My teacher jokingly called me "the Butcher." I was mortified every time she called on me, but I pushed through.

Math, on the other hand, I avoided like the plague — until I couldn't anymore. Still, the college had a laid-back vibe, and I genuinely enjoyed my classes. Once I gained confidence, I enrolled in two courses each semester. I studied during the day while the kids were at school. By the time they came home, I had put my books away and helped them with their homework.

As long as I stayed organized, I managed to keep everything on track. I was finding my rhythm and beginning to believe in myself. Then the community college became a State College, and everything changed. Suddenly, five-page papers replaced two-page reports, and the workload intensified. I struggled to keep up.

Worse, my old enemy returned: test anxiety. No matter how much I prepared, I froze during exams. Even multiple-choice questions tripped me up. Once, I thought I had done well — until I got my test back and saw a giant red zero. Panicked, I checked my answers and realized I had filled in the wrong bubbles throughout.

After class, I approached the teacher, mortified. Thankfully, he was understanding and shifted all my answers up by one. I ended up with a B, but I was still upset, so I called my mother to vent.

"Why are you putting yourself through this?" she asked. "You're married with a family. You don't need college."

For a moment, I almost agreed. Her words felt like permission to quit. But they also stirred something deep inside me — memories of high school counselors who told me I wasn't college material. If I gave up now, they'd be right. I couldn't let that happen. I wasn't just doing this for a degree — I was doing it to prove I could.

The days felt relentless. No matter how fast I moved, I never seemed to get ahead. Every morning, I prepared for class. Every afternoon, I would pick up the kids and stop at the store for dinner. One evening, the temperature had dropped since I'd left home. I rummaged through the trunk and found a sweater.

As I rushed around the supermarket, Annmarie and Jason lagged behind.

"Come on," I said. "I've got a ton of homework. No time to play."

They just giggled.

"What's so funny?" I finally asked, turning to look at them.

And there it was — the source of their amusement. One of Jason's socks was stuck to my sleeve, held there by an uneaten, cherry-flavored lollipop. Sticky strings of goo trailed as I tried to pull the sock off.

"Ew!" Annmarie squealed, wrinkling her nose.

"Thanks a lot, guys!" I couldn't help laughing either. It was ridiculous, chaotic, and quintessentially *me*. Typical of my life.

Chapter 23 | Doggie Jail

Michael took a job at an exhibit company — a real job with health insurance and vacation pay. With our finances finally on steadier ground, I felt more at ease about the future. I was grateful for the security and stability his job brought, but it left him no time to work on the house. His tools lay right where he left them.

One afternoon, I stepped on a chisel Michael had left on the floor. Blood spurted across the tile.

"Ew!" Jason said and scrunched his nose. "I'll get you a Band-Aid, Mommy!" He ran to the bathroom, and despite the pain, I couldn't help but smile.

"Thank you, sweetheart. I don't know what I would do without you."

"Mommy? Can we get another dog?"

After a German Shepherd attacked our Poodle, I hadn't had the heart to consider it. But I couldn't say no to Jason.

The next day, while he was at school, I took a ride to the County animal shelter. Even before I opened the door, I could hear the barking dogs inside.

"I'm looking to adopt a puppy," I told the girl behind the counter.

"Right through there," she said, pointing to a set of double doors.

The sound of yelping led me into a large, dimly lit warehouse. I walked slowly down one row after another, peeking into each cage, but they were all filled with large dogs. No puppies. Disappointed, I was about to leave when I spotted a medium-sized dog with sad, brown eyes. His cage was far too small. He could barely turn around.

"Can you tell me about this one?" I asked an attendant.

He pulled out the card and read the information on the back. "Chow mix. Picked up last month. Someone abandoned him at the end of a road. He was skittish when they brought him in. He's scheduled to be put to sleep this week."

"Put to sleep?" I repeated, horrified.

He nodded. "We can only hold them for so long. If they're not adopted, they get euthanized."

I signed the adoption papers, and Jason had his dog.

The dog lay curled in the corner of the kitchen, shivering with fear. But the moment Jason walked through the front door, he came to life, rushing over to smother him with wet kisses. It was the perfect scene — a boy and his dog.

"Buffy!" Jason declared. "That's his name."

"Isn't that a girl's … " I hesitated, then smiled. "That's a great name."

"Come on, Buffy! Let's go play!"

That night, Buffy began making strange gagging sounds. It was clear he was sick. He coughed constantly, expelling green mucus and struggling to breathe. The veterinarian diagnosed him with kennel cough and prescribed medication. The treatment made his fur fall out, leaving him bald. I cried, afraid I had made a terrible mistake. He was the ugliest dog I had ever seen, but Jason never gave up on him. He even slept beside him on the floor.

Over time, Buffy recovered. His coat grew back thick and rich, a beautiful brown. He was a stunning dog. He preferred cat food over dog food, but most days, he just ate table food.

People often say Chows are vicious, yet Buffy was gentle and sweet—just wary of men. He tolerated the cats, even when Riley smacked him or Gizmo, our white Persian, rubbed against him. One day, I found them napping side by side. I called them Beauty and the Beast.

Buffy sat peacefully in the yard, content to watch me work in the garden. When the phone rang, I slipped off my gloves and went inside. It was my sister Carol. By the time we finished chatting, I no longer felt like digging in the dirt. Instead, I headed upstairs to take a shower.

A sudden knock at the front door made me jump. I hadn't heard a car pull into the driveway. I peeked outside. A police officer stood on the porch.

"May I help you?" I asked, stepping outside.

"Do you own a brown dog?"

My stomach dropped. I had forgotten Buffy was still outside. "Is he all right?"

"He's fine, ma'am—but the kid he bit isn't."

"Buffy bit someone?" My voice rose in disbelief. "Is it serious?"

"I'm not sure. The parents called to report it. They haven't pressed charges, but he needs to be quarantined for ten days to make sure he doesn't have rabies."

"Can't I keep him here? I'll make sure he stays inside."

"Sorry, ma'am. I have to take him. It's the law."

"What if I board him at a kennel for ten days?"

He hesitated. "I'll have to request authorization."

"Okay," he said after speaking to someone on his radio. "But I have to take him there myself."

I rushed inside to call the kennel and was relieved to find they had room. I jotted down the address and handed it to the officer.

"Here's the name and location."

He loaded Buffy into the back of the patrol car. "Don't worry, ma'am. He'll be fine."

"Can I get the phone number of the boy's parents? I'd like to check on him."

He scribbled a name and number onto his notepad and handed it to me.

After he left, I called the parents. The husband admitted their son had kicked Buffy. That's when the dog bit him on the calf. They said the bite was minor and that the boy was fine, but his wife wanted to report it.

When I arrived at the kennel, Buffy jumped up and ran to the front of the cage, tail wagging, ready to be set free.

"Sorry, boy. You have to stay a little longer."

I left him a soft pillow, a few cans of dog food, and some chew toys. I even paid extra so he could get out of the cage once a day and run in the large, fenced-in yard behind the building. Leaving him was heartbreaking, but at least I could visit.

For ten days, I checked on him like clockwork. I sat outside the kennel while he stretched his legs and soaked up the sun. He always looked confused when it was time to go back into the cage. Once, after I closed the door behind me, I heard him barking, and it broke my heart.

Finally, the ordeal was over for both of us. On the ride home, I rolled down the window, and Buffy stuck his head out, ears flapping in the breeze.

Chapter 24 | Peachtree

The aroma of tomato sauce filled the kitchen, transporting me back to childhood. The sizzle of meatballs frying in the skillet filled the air, just as it had every Sunday growing up. My mother always made "gravy" in the old pot passed down from her mother. She'd hold two meatballs for my father — he liked them without sauce. Catering to his every whim, she even made a lamb shank just for him. Although I loved Sunday dinners, I resented how my mother would often spend the entire day in the kitchen. And yet, here I was, committed to the same ritual.

Buffy sat at my feet, watching every move as I mixed the meatball ingredients. Now and then, I would toss him a piece of raw chopped meat, which he would catch midair.

My choice to become a wife and stay-at-home mom had once felt safe — secure in its predictability. I was comfortable, if not content, in a life of quiet subservience. I put a pot of water on the stove for the pasta and glanced at the clock. Michael was two hours late.

I set a dish aside for him and called the kids to the table. We ate together without saying much. Just as I was wiping down the counter, I heard the door open. Michael stepped inside. Something in his demeanor felt off.

Without a word, I unwrapped the plate I had left on the stove and set it on the table for him.

"Christmas is coming soon," I said to the kids, trying to sound cheerful.

"Can we get a big Christmas tree this year?" Jason asked.

"The biggest!" I replied.

"Are we going to have lots of presents?"

"Of course! And cookies, and candies, and a big turkey."

"I can't wait!" Annmarie shouted. "I'm going to start my list for Santa after dinner."

"Me too!" Jason said, finishing his food in record time.

"Slow down. Don't eat so fast." I smiled.

The kids dashed off to make their wish lists, and I turned back to Michael. He had a strange look on his face.

"What's wrong?"

"I quit my job today," he said flatly.

My smile vanished. "What?"

"They brought in some big shot from Chicago to take over. I've been running that shop for months. Now they want to demote me to a laborer. They can kiss my ass."

"But... why'd you have to quit?"

"I'll find something else. Don't worry about it."

But I did worry. As I cleared the table, the warmth of the evening faded, replaced by a sinking feeling in my gut.

Life was about to get harder.

After two weeks without a job, our financial situation was dire. There were no savings to fall back on. I gathered the presents I had carefully wrapped and hidden for Christmas and returned them so I could buy groceries, but that didn't go very far.

The supermarket had always been my refuge, a legitimate place to escape my daily stresses. I'd walk the aisles planning the dinners I intended to cook without the guilt of spending money. I wandered around aimlessly among the broccoli and peaches, looking for produce on sale.

Staying along the outer edges of the supermarket, I lingered in the meat department. It sure would be nice to buy a thick, juicy steak for dinner, I thought, picking up each package and examining the marbling of the beef. I settled for chicken.

Lately, that's all we seemed to eat—fried, baked, stir-fried, or barbequed.

For the first time, I noticed how many men accompanied their wives. Eavesdropping on their conversations, I was surprised at how much the men shared in decisions. I wondered what it would be like to have a husband like that. Michael rarely stepped into a store. I don't ever remember us shopping together.

Edward was watching television as I struggled to get the grocery bags from the trunk.

"I had a panic attack today," I huffed.

"Why?"

"I had to use the credit card to buy food. I couldn't catch my breath. When are you going to find a job?"

"I'm doing the best I can. No one is hiring right now."

"Can't you ask for your job back? They'll probably hire you if you apologize."

"No! I won't give them the satisfaction."

"Then, why don't we sell the house and move back to Long Island — or Florida? At least we have family there. Maybe they can help you find work."

"It's out of the question."

Engrossed in his show, he took a bite of an apple. The juice collected in the corner of his mouth, and the crunching of his jaw irritated me. I could barely look at him without feeling resentment. Lately, everything about him made me want to jump out the window — the sound of his voice, how he slurped his coffee, and even how he smelled.

"What are we going to do?"

"Maybe I can go into business for myself. I know about conventions. We can use the den as an office, and I'll build a garage with a workshop and work from home."

"Where do you plan to get the money for this venture?"

"Well, we can refinance the house."

"You want to use our equity? That's risky?"

"Adding a garage will increase the value of the house. Besides, I'll be making so much money that we may be able to buy a better house next year."

Michael always knew how to manipulate me. I signed the document to refinance our mortgage.

Chapter 25 | Sunshine State

Annmarie ran into the house and sulked.

"What's wrong, honey?"

"Lily isn't allowed to play with me."

"Why?"

"She says I'm a Yankee."

"Do you want me to call her mother?"

"Yes," Annmarie sobbed.

"Okay. Don't worry. For now, play with your brother."

When Annmarie went outside, I picked up the phone and dialed the neighbor's number.

"Hi Ellen, it's Florence. Annmarie says Lily isn't allowed to play with her. Did something happen?"

"Bless her heart," Ellen said. "I don't know where she got that idea."

"Maybe she misunderstood. Can Lily come over tomorrow?"

There was a pause. "Lily has to go to a birthday party," she replied.

"Oh," I said, but I sensed she was making an excuse. When I hung up, I stood by the kitchen window, lost in thought, remembering the sting of losing my own childhood friend, Jessica.

We had met through a neighbor. She had three sisters, one brother, and parents who ran their house like clockwork—from study time to bedtime. They were the kind of structured family every child secretly aspires to have. Dinner was always at the same time, and church was non-negotiable on Sundays. I wished my family had been more like that.

Sometimes, Jessica invited me to sleep over. On Saturdays, we'd hop on the bus that ran along Broadway to Jones Beach or the mall. One Friday afternoon, looking forward to the weekend, I called her house. Our wall phone had an extra-long cord, so I took it into the hall closet—my makeshift phone booth. I slipped into the darkness among the winter coats, breathing in the musty scent of mothballs.

"Is Stacy there?"

"Who's this?" her mother asked.

"Florence."

"Oh, hold on."

I could hear muffled voices in the background as I waited. Finally, Jessica got on.

"Florence, I can't talk to you now," she whispered, her voice barely audible over the pounding in my ears.

"What's wrong?"

"My father doesn't want me to hang around with you anymore."

"Why?"

"I think it's because you're from the city."

"What's that got to do with anything?"

"He thinks you're a bad influence. He's weird. I'll see you at school. Save me a seat in the lunchroom tomorrow."

The line went dead, but I stood there in the closet until the sharp beep of the dial tone jolted me. A bad influence? If anyone was a bad influence, it was Jessica. She smoked cigarettes and stole vodka from her parents' liquor cabinet. I wondered if she had gotten caught and blamed me. After that, I was never allowed to sleep over again. If we wanted to hang out, I had to hide down the block.

Parents can be crueler than kids, I thought. Now my daughter was facing the same rejection. I couldn't let the neighborhood destroy her happiness the way mine had been chipped away. I just wanted my children to fit in, but the damn neighbors wouldn't give them a chance. If I didn't come up with something, it was going to be a long, miserable summer.

So, I joined the new water park. Every day, I packed up our lunches, and we jumped in the car. Every day, I sat under a canopy, working on my cross-stitch while the kids played in the water. It was a peaceful time—pushing a silver needle in and out of the fabric, coaxing tiny flowers to bloom beneath my fingertips.

I tried to maintain the image of the happy homemaker, but since Michael began working from home, I was miserable.

The holidays crept up again, and though everyone else seemed to be in a better mood, I wasn't. It's not easy pretending that everything is all right in your life just because you are expected to be joyous. This time of year always made me more homesick.

As a child, Christmas meant that cousins, aunts, and uncles would gather, creating a sense of joy and belonging.

Now, far from my childhood home, Christmas felt empty. Still, I was determined to give my kids something worth remembering. I baked cookies while holiday music filled the house.

I'll be home for Christmas… You can count on me…

As I sang along, tears welled in my eyes.

"Why are you crying, Mommy?" Jason asked.

"I want to go home," I sniffled.

"You are home," he said, tilting his head in confusion.

His words struck me. *Where was home? Brooklyn? Long Island?*

Georgia certainly didn't feel like it. No matter how long I lived there, I was always an outsider. The realization that nothing tied me to this place made me ache with longing.

I wondered where I truly wanted to be for the holidays. My mother and sister were in Florida. That was it. That's where I wanted to be for Christmas.

"I'd like to go to Florida for Christmas," I told Michael when he came home from work.

"We already bought our tree," he said.

"Yes, but the kids are off from school for two weeks, and I want to visit my mother. The exhibit business is slow this time of year. You could take some time off."

WELCOME TO FLORIDA.

We crossed the Georgia-Florida line, and the sun came out; my mood instantly lifted. Between bathroom breaks and hunger pangs, we inched our way toward my mother's house.

With three hours to go, Michael stopped for gas. I jumped out and grabbed a free local paper. As we reentered the highway, I flipped through the classifieds.

"Look! There's a two-bedroom townhouse for sale nearby. It's just like my mother's. Wouldn't it be nice if we could buy it?"

"You're always complaining that we have no money, and now you want to buy a townhouse? That's your problem. You live beyond your means. That's why we're always broke."

"It's not like I'm buying jewelry and fancy cars," I said defensively.

"You never save, either," he snapped. "Why can't you be like my brother's wife? She's frugal."

Frugal. The word buzzed in my ear like a fly.

I hated the sound of it almost as much as the word *wholesome*. Wholesome and frugal—two things I would never be.

I turned back toward the window, letting the lush Florida greenery soothe my disappointment. At least I would be spending the holidays with my mother.

While Michael took the children fishing, she and I shared quiet time over coffee—just the two of us.

I confided to her that school was stressful and I was having a hard time keeping up. Of course, she suggested that I quit, just as Michael had. I learned to stop complaining.

Chapter 26 | Au François

There was a rumor that my small-town college would be elevated to university status within the next few years. I couldn't put it off any longer—I had to take math.

On the first day of algebra, I sat in the front row, determined to face my fear head-on. The teacher began writing figures on the board. At first, it made sense—until it didn't. It all fell apart so quickly. The other students, fresh out of high school, followed along with ease, while I sat frozen, pretending to take notes. After class, I marched straight to the office and requested a transfer to pre-algebra.

The next day, I walked into the same classroom with a fresh start—or so I hoped. But the same teacher began scribbling on the board, and almost instantly, I was lost again. It was like an out-of-body experience, watching myself drift further from comprehension with every equation. It was painfully clear that the math was still over my head. I didn't belong there, so I dropped out of the class.

The temptation to drop out of school overwhelmed me.

When I mentioned it to Michael, he perked up. "Quit!" he said, as if I had just offered to lighten his load. "It's not like you're going to become the president or something. You don't need a degree."

Maybe he was right. If I quit, I'd have more time for my family. That would make Michael happy. But what about me? I'd feel like a failure. His words were a slap in the face — but in a good way. They snapped me out of my spiral. I wasn't ready to give up.

Summer was just around the corner, so I made a plan. I bought an algebra textbook and decided to teach myself one chapter at a time. I carried it everywhere, even on a camping trip to the mountains. While Michael set up the tent and took the kids on a hike, I found the perfect spot for my hammock — nestled between two trees — and began studying.

By the time the fall semester arrived, I was able to hold my own. I squeaked by with a C and moved on to the next class. Somewhere along the way, math started to make sense. The tutor my father hired when I was a little girl hadn't been a waste after all. When I got an A in Calculus, I was ecstatic. I couldn't wait to tell my dad.

That small victory lit something inside me. A spark. I wanted more. With each passing semester, my confidence grew.

One morning, I noticed a familiar car behind me as I drove to the university. It was my neighbor Tami. She was probably heading to work — a job she openly despised. Two miles down the road, I turned left at the light and glanced in the mirror. She was still behind me. When I pulled into the school parking lot, she followed and parked just a few spaces away from me.

She stepped out of her car with a bounce in her step. "What are you doing here?" I asked.

"I signed up for college," she said with a proud grin. "You inspired me. I guess we're going to be classmates."

My stomach twisted. Tami's decision to enroll was unexpected — and unsettling. Her new academic journey became a mirror reflecting all my insecurities. I had finally found something that made me feel good about myself, and now here she was, about to walk the same path. *She'll be better at it,* I thought. But then a quieter voice pushed back. *It's not a competition. So what if Tami does better? I'm not doing this for anyone but myself.* I took a breath and pushed the doubt aside.

While waiting for class to start, I wandered down the hallway, skimming the bulletin board plastered with flyers. One of them caught my eye — a bold, colorful ad for a study abroad program in Paris. I tore it off and tucked it into my purse.

Paris! Even the name made my heart flutter. Ever since junior high, I had been obsessed with all things French. We had a visiting French teacher — young, stylish, with a melodic accent — and I clung to every word. But halfway through the semester, I was moved from the Regents program to a lower track. Just like that, no more French.

Years later, my friend Cindy and I took a trip to France when we were twenty-three. We had a great time, but it would've been so much better if we'd known the language. Now, with three years of college French under my belt, I was eager to dive back in — to live, learn, and absorb it all.

I had spent the last eighteen years as a full-time mom, raising two children and helping Michael run our business. Somewhere in all that giving, I had lost parts of myself. But now, here was a chance — a two-month study abroad program in Paris. *When will I ever have the opportunity like this again?*

Still, I couldn't help but worry. How could I leave? Like it or not, I was the glue that held everything together. Even though the kids were old enough to take care of themselves. My classes had already stretched his patience over the years.

Convincing Michael wouldn't be easy, but that evening at dinner, I found the perfect opportunity.

"What do you want for your birthday?" he asked.

"Funny you should ask." I reached into my purse and pulled out the flyer. The college is offering a study abroad program in Paris. I want to sign up."

His face tightened. "Who's going to work in the office?"

"It's not until next summer," I said quickly. "That's your slow season. And besides, Annmarie and Jason are old enough to help out."

After a long pause, he said, "Okay."

Just like that, it was real. I was going to Paris.

Filled with a mix of anticipation and anxiety, I packed my bags and set off for the City of Light. For the first time in years, I felt a sense of freedom.

Chapter 27 | Paris Adventure

As soon as I arrived in Paris, I was enveloped by a sense of independence that I hadn't felt in years. Sitting on the bus among the other students, I stared out of the window, soaking in the city's beauty, its layers of history. It was even more breathtaking than the first time I visited Paris with my friend Cindy.

The bus pulled up in front of the Jean Monnet FIAP—an international student residence in the 14th arrondissement. I was assigned a small shared room that felt more like a cubicle, just big enough for a single bed and a desk. Each unit housed two students, and I was lucky enough to arrive first and claim the bed by the window.

From there, I looked down onto the garden courtyard where students gathered to eat and socialize in a dozen different languages. I was the oldest student in the group, but I didn't mind. In fact, I welcomed the separation—it gave me space to experience Paris on my own terms.

That night, I left my window open to feel the cool night breeze. Puffy white clouds drifted past a sky filled with stars. One by one, the apartment lights in the distance blinked off until only blackness remained. I lay there, lulled to sleep by the sounds.

The next morning, Paris sparkled. I walked to the corner bakery and bought pain au chocolat, the first of many small indulgences.

After class, I wandered the winding streets of the Marais, pausing to admire the hidden boutiques tucked into narrow alleys. I bought a crêpe from a vendor wearing a red beret and made my way to Shakespeare and Company. I ran my fingers along the spines of books that had been loved for generations. Surrounded by stories, I felt like I belonged.

Paris was just as beautiful as I remembered from my last trip, bursting with possibility — but I moved through it with a different motivation. This time, I wasn't searching for love in every smile or romanticizing every café corner.

I carried my books to nearby parks, where I read or wrote in my journal — a requirement for the travel abroad program. I'd sit on a bench for hours, watching couples stroll hand-in-hand, and children chase soccer balls across the lawn. Sometimes I took the metro to sit beneath the Eiffel Tower with a book, or found a quiet café to sip coffee and simply observe. Though I felt lonely at times, I was also discovering what it meant to be on my own — with no roles, no titles, no expectations.

The phone line in the FIAP lobby was always long. I waited patiently, calling home every few days. It was my only tether to the world I had left behind.

Back in Georgia, life had been full of obligations. Here, time felt suspended. I let myself exist in the quiet. While many of the other students spent weekends partying or taking road trips to neighboring countries, I didn't want to waste a single moment of my time away from Paris.

My days were filled with language classes and field trips to the city. I immersed myself in geography, history, and culture. I visited the Catacombs—just a few blocks from our residence. At first, I felt brave walking through alone, but halfway in, a wave of unease hit me. I picked up my pace and rushed through the tunnel, emerging with white dust clinging to my shoes. Was it bone dust? The thought made me queasy.

One afternoon, I decided to visit Père Lachaise Cemetery. Jim Morrison was buried there, and The Doors had been my favorite band as a teenager. I eventually found his grave, but it saddened me. The headstone had been defaced with graffiti, and the top stone had been stolen. It felt like a forgotten shrine, vandalized and unprotected.

Evenings became my favorite time in Paris. After dinner in the FIAP cafeteria, I often wandered along the Seine for hours, letting the city wrap around me like a silk gown. One night, as I was preparing to head out, a black girl approached and asked where I was going. When I told her, she asked if she could join me. Her name was Danielle, also from Georgia.

I'd never had a black friend before. Back in New York, the few black students I knew had been bused in from different neighborhoods. There was always tension. Some of the girls were openly hostile, and I'd had my share of run-ins. But Danielle was different. She smiled easily and was studying to become a nurse. We walked together that evening — and many evenings after that. She became my first real friend of color, and I was grateful for the bond we formed.

When it was time to go home, I boarded the plane with a bittersweet ache. I was eager to see my family and pets, but I knew part of my soul would remain in Paris.

Chapter 28 | College Material

Since the college converted from a state college to a university, I often found myself in tears. The workload was heavier, and I had to study more. Hanging on for dear life, I only had one more year. Michael didn't make things any easier. He confronted me with yet another business disaster.

"We need to get another loan from the bank," he said. "I underestimated the cost of a job."

"How much money are you short?"

"About five thousand dollars."

"We can't keep taking money out of the house. I knew having our own business was a bad idea."

"You're overreacting again, Florence."

"I'll sign on one condition," I said. "You need to rent a warehouse. It's not working with both of us at home. Besides, you'll be more focused if you have an office."

"I'll look for one, but we have to go to the bank tomorrow."

"I can't. I have a class in the morning."

"Maybe if you dropped out of school, you would have more time to help get this business off the ground."

For a brief moment, the voices in my head agreed with Michael. It would make my life less hectic, but a flicker of resistance stirred within me.

"No," I said. "I'm not quitting."

The sky was heavy with black clouds mirroring the tension I carried inside. I rushed home from the office and poured myself a glass of wine. Lately, I relied on it more than I should have, and the thought of becoming an alcoholic like my father loomed. I pushed away the thought and stood in front of the open refrigerator, wondering if I had enough vegetables to make a stir-fry. A drop of water hit my shoulder, and then another. I looked up at the kitchen ceiling, swollen with water. It was going to burst at any moment. *Michael promised to fix that pipe!*

My annoyance bubbled up. I was tired—tired of broken promises and unfinished projects. Michael no longer had an interest in the house. He never finished one project before moving on to another. When he had to put on his tool belt, he'd be in a foul mood for days.

The marble floor was starting to yellow. Michael had warned me not to spend the money on marble, claiming that it was hard to maintain and could discolor, but I didn't listen. Now, I didn't want to give him any reason to chastise me for my decision. It took so little to send him spinning out of control, and the slightest amount of pressure made him lose his composure.

My mother was by my side on graduation day. It was one of those rare moments between mother and daughter, and I was glad to have her witness my achievements. She was proud that I had made it to the end. I'd had doubts. I applied for a position at the Canadian Consulate in Atlanta, equipped with my bachelor's degree and four years of French studies. I dreamed of working at the U.N. in New York City. Once I had enough experience, I'd have options.

Just as I was preparing for a new chapter, the convention business was taking off, and the client list kept growing. Michael needed me to run the exhibit business, so I put my dreams on hold and took the corner office, where I hung my diploma above my desk. It was proof that the high school counselor was wrong. I was college material!

Chapter 29 | Buffy Boy

When Jason first requested a dog, I was hesitant. I'd never been a dog person. Still, I grew attached as the years went by. We celebrated Buffy's birthday on Thanksgiving and gave him as much turkey as he could eat. I'd wrap dog bones and toys at Christmas and place them under the tree. Buffy would sneak into the living room and grab one or two of his presents when no one was looking.

Now that the kids were older, they were rarely home. Buffy filled the lonely gap. I'd take him for a walk around the neighborhood every evening, and he'd prance down the street like a show horse, tail high and steps springy. As he grew older, arthritis began to take over his body. He could only walk a few blocks before stopping. Even when I took his leash off so he could run free, he just stood there. I had noticed a change in him. He could sense a storm coming even before any signs of it. He would rip the Sheetrock off the walls, trying to escape. He stopped eating and had no energy. The vet reminded me that he was sixteen. There was no magic pill, but I wasn't ready to let him go. I set up a mattress in the garage. He'd lie there and look out the window, surrounded by his pillows and toys.

One morning, Buffy came to my bed, whining. I knew he was in trouble. As we drove to the vet, the dog stared out the window and panted. The doctor examined him and said he was in pain. There was nothing we could do except euthanize him. I couldn't do it. Michael was in the kitchen when I got home. "The vet says we should euthanize Buffy."

"He's sixteen years old. If he's sick, it's probably best. I'll take him. Help me put him in my truck."

I kissed Buffy goodbye with a heavy heart and watched him leave, knowing it was the last time I'd see him."

A few hours later, Michael came home with Buffy's body so we could bury him in the yard. We dug a hole under a canopy of trees.

After placing the cardboard box wth my beloved dog into a shallow hole, I drove to the store to buy a white Rhododendron to mark his grave. The plant grew and sheltered him from the rain as its roots wrapped around him like a blanket. Knowing he was one with the earth, his life force taking a new shape, gave me solace. When the blooms were in season, they were like a gentle hello from Buffy.

Chapter 30 | Bad Design

My eardrums pounded as Michael's motorcycle came up the driveway. My temper was reaching the boiling point. I shook my head and thought, *not a care in the world.* When he bought his first bike, I didn't say anything. A second, then a third, sat in the garage, adding to his collection. *Where's he getting money for these motorcycles?*

Shaking it off, I turned away from the window and set the table in the patio room.

When Annmarie announced she was getting married, I tried to talk her out of it. I had hoped she wouldn't follow the same path I had, but the thought of being a homemaker appealed to her.

Jason went away to college in Colorado. He lasted only one semester before returning to Georgia, where he moved into an apartment instead of going home.

My days as a homemaker came to an end, and I lost my sense of purpose. I didn't know how to face the world without being a Mom.

Dinner passed in silence.

"I'm going back to the office to finish some bookkeeping and check the mail," I said. "Can you clean the kitchen?"

"Yeah, put everything in the sink."

I preferred to do most of my work at night when the office was empty. I backed out of our driveway, carefully avoiding the potholes, and put the house behind me.

When I arrived at the warehouse, the parking lot was empty except for my car. The only light shining in the secluded office park was mine, and every sound made me jump. I opened the mail, wrote out checks, and recorded them on the computer. As the funds in our bank account decreased, my anxiety increased. I sat for a moment with my elbows on the desk and my head in my hands.

It was almost midnight. I couldn't see straight. I shut off the light, plunging me into darkness. Inching along the wall, I used the illuminated exit sign as my guide. Outside, I looked to see that no one was lurking in the bushes and locked the door. Tired and emotionally drained, I drove home.

Michael didn't clean the kitchen, like he promised. I grumbled and went upstairs to bed.

The next day, I went to Home Depot for a can of paint. Listening to music while I painted the walls, I was like a kid with a new box of crayons. The fresh smell of paint was heady. In only my underwear and one of Michael's old shirts, I stepped up on the ladder and started cutting in the edges. It took a steady hand, but I inched around the room, moving the ladder and the paint can as I went along. The walls absorbed the paint, filling in cracks and holes as if to hide the neglect. It wasn't perfect, but I wasn't striving for perfection — only change.

Michael's motorcycle pulled into the driveway. He's home, I thought, and quickly closed the paint can, knowing how he felt whenever I started a new project.

He walked into the bathroom and stared at the walls. "What the heck are you doing? It looks terrible."

"At least I try. When was the last time you picked up a paintbrush?"

"Sorry, it's …. Well, we have different ideas about decorating, that's all."

"What does that mean?"

"It's a terrible color, for one thing. Face it. You've always been a lousy decorator!"

The blood rushed to my face. It was as if he had said I was ugly or stupid. No, it was worse.

"I hate you, Michael, and I hate this house!"

I'd always chosen my words carefully to avoid the risk of making him angry in the past.

Searching for something to destroy, my eyes focused on the wallpaper in the hall. I had thought it looked nice when I found it at the hardware store, but after Michael hung it on the wall, the pattern was too large for such a small space.

"I'm not taking it down," he had warned, sensing my dissatisfaction.

The wallpaper stood before me as a symbol of my concessions to keep the peace. Forced to live with it, my punishment for bad taste, I didn't say anything. I ran to the wall and worked my fingers under the seams that had separated over time, tearing at the worn wallpaper with my bare hands. With every rip, I released some of my frustration. I moved down the hall to the stairway.

Michael slipped out the side door, but I didn't notice. I sat sobbing on the stairs. Streams of wallpaper hung down as I stared at the mess I had made. I'd wasted years — years of painting, wallpapering, and yard work. Chores were better suited to a carpenter or a handyman. The house had become an obsession, an anchor in a sea of despair. Feeling like a mouse in an endless maze, I couldn't go back. I couldn't go forward either. My dream house had become a nightmare.

My marriage was in shambles, but I clung to my existence like a comfortable pair of worn slippers.

I laid a towel across the gaping crack at the bottom of the back door to block the draft and prevent the heat from escaping. The house no longer brought me joy as it continued to fall further into disrepair, but I held onto the hope that things would change. Maybe that was the problem. Hope paralyzed me, preventing me from making changes in my life.

"When are you going to fix the pipe in the ceiling?" I asked Michael.

"When you stop nagging me!"

"Nag? Is that what I do?"

"You're always nagging."

"If you did what you were supposed to, I wouldn't have to nag."

Rummaging through the cabinet, Michael pulled out a large pot and handed it to me.

"What am I supposed to do with this?"

"Put it under the leak," he snapped.

My house had become a prison, and Michael was the warden.

Living with him was like a life sentence with no parole for good behavior. *Some couples are soulmates, but we're cellmates.*

Chapter 31 | Twin Towers

The attacks on the World Trade Center triggered Michael, and his behavior became unpredictable.

Major businesses canceled exhibiting events, and the only income we had was from storage. We could no longer hold onto the warehouse, so Michael brought the warehouse home. Once more, I had to sign for an equity loan so he could build a facility on our land. Against my wishes, he built a two-story structure in front of the living room windows, claiming it was the only place suitable. Resentful, I felt the tension between us increase. Conversation ceased between Michael and me as a relentless war of passive aggression replaced words.

The smallest things caused conflict. One of these was the ceiling fan in our bedroom. I'd wake up sweaty and realize it was off, so I jumped out of bed and flipped it on.

"I shut that," he mumbled.

"I'm going through menopause," I said and flipped the switch. "I can't sleep without a fan."

An hour later, I woke up in a cold sweat. "Why do you keep shutting the fan?"

"The swishing reminds me of Vietnam."

"It never bothered you before."

"Yes, it did. I just never mentioned it."

The next night, I faced the same problem. I flipped on the fan. At three am, it was off. On — off-on--off. The game continued, shifting to other topics, such as the porch light. I always left the switch on at night. Every day, he flipped the switch off on his way out the door.

"It's a sensor light. It shuts off by itself when the sun comes out," I explained. I even tried taping the switch on in protest, but nothing worked.

I walked around the house, picking up plastic, wood, and nails, and carried four cans of paint with rusted tops and two heavy ladders into the shop. Tools and debris littered the driveway. The smell of grease and dirty linens mingled with the breeze flowing through the open window.

"Keep out of the warehouse," Michael warned.

"I wouldn't have to go in there if you put your tools away."

"Next time, ask."

"Do you have something to hide?"

Tempted to stand my ground, I shrugged and agreed to stay out of his man cave.

Michael refused to apply for an electrical permit, stating it was none of the government's business and they just wanted money. He set up a bed on the top floor of the warehouse. Over the years, he'd occasionally camped outside, but this seemed more permanent. Like a bear, he hibernated for the winter. He spent most of his time in the garage, and I was never sure he was home. Since there was no electrical source in the warehouse, Michael ran an extension cord from the garage, snaking it through a side window.

I pulled the plug.

"Hey, I'm working in here," he'd yell.

I rolled my eyes and plugged the cord back into the socket.

If Michael came into the house, it was only to grab a cup of coffee or a snack. I was surprised when he came in for dinner one night. Thank goodness for the television. It helped to alleviate the awkwardness.

That night, I awoke to the sound of loud sawing. Burying my head under the pillow only dulled the noise. I ran outside barefoot, pausing to peel a screw off the sole of my left heel. Luckily, the point wasn't sticking straight up and didn't break the skin. I hobbled to the warehouse and pulled aside the plastic sheet he had stapled over the doorway to keep the heat in.

"What are you doing, Michael? It's the middle of the night!"

"You're letting the cold air in," he complained. "Go back to bed."

I left the plastic sheet blowing in the wind and returned to my room.

The next day, a letter was in the mailbox.

"Dear neighbor, I lost sleep last night due to your sawing and hammering until 2 a.m. This is unacceptable. Either you are unaware of the county noise ordinance, or you are simply an inconsiderate person. I have never complained that you run a manufacturing business in a residential area with trucks coming and going during the day. I figured you were making an honest living. However, please keep me from doing the same with no sleep. If you wake my family again after 10 p.m., I'll have to report you to the county zoning board. They'll shut you down immediately."

The minute Michael came through the door, I tossed the letter at him. "I knew it was only a matter of time before the neighbors started complaining. Now, we're going to have the county after us."

"Stop overreacting—he won't report us."

"How do you know that?"

"I'll take care of it. Just leave. Go visit your mom in Florida!"

"Maybe I will!"

The next day, I drove out of the neighborhood with its perfectly maintained houses and manicured lawns.

Holding Back the Years by Simply Red played on the car radio. My foot trembled on the gas pedal as my eyes filled with tears.

I'll keep holding on.

Tears trickled down my cheeks, slow at first, but soon, I sobbed.

Nothing had the chance to be good. Nothing ever could, yeah.

I shut off the radio, but the lyrics were still in my head. Reaching for my cell phone, I called my girlfriend, Janine. Like me, she had been a stay-at-home mom. After twenty-eight years of marriage, her husband asked for a divorce. He left her penniless. She didn't know how to support herself.

"I can't stand it anymore," I cried. "Michael reeks of pot and motorcycle grease. All he does is stay in the warehouse he built with sixties music blasting."

"At least he didn't run off with his secretary like Bill."

"Michael doesn't have a secretary. I do all the paperwork. It's not easy, either. I have to beg him for receipts. He keeps them in his wallet for months. By the time I get them, they're old and curled. It takes forever to sort them. Sometimes, he puts them in his pants pocket, and they disappear in the wash. We will likely be audited someday. I just know it! I think about it in the middle of the night. It's no wonder I can't sleep. On top of that, he has the nerve to tell me the business is his, not mine."

"Women never get credit in a man's business."

"I think he's burnt out from all that pot he smokes. I did tell you about the pot plant I found in the yard, right?"

"No! Is Michael growing pot behind the house?"

"Yes. First, he hid it among the tomatoes. I told him to get rid of it, or I would. He said I was overreacting, but he pulled it out."

"Good. You could lose your house. Oh, Florence, this is serious. Maybe you should leave him."

"I want to leave him, but if we get divorced, I'll have to sell everything, including the house."

"It's not fair, but is it worth being unhappy for the rest of your life?"

"I don't know anymore. I've been in pain for so long. I'm numb."

"Think about it, and let's get together for lunch next week."

"Okay, thanks for listening."

I flipped my cell phone closed. Janine was right, of course. I had become fixated on holding onto the house. It prevented me from facing reality.

Chapter 32 | Monkey Business

As the months flew by, money was tight. Ever since the fall of the Twin Towers, our clients had scaled back their exhibits. Some even pulled out of the shows. Michael rarely showed up at the office, which left me to work in peace.

Michael pulled up on his motorcycle and killed the engine. I waited for him to enter, but he sneaked past my office without saying a word.

I jumped up to confront him. "Where have you been?" I demanded, though I knew he'd been riding his motorcycle all morning.

"I had something to take care of."

"I can't run this business by myself."

"No one expects you to."

"Why don't you start making sales calls?"

"You're a real bitch! You know that?" He headed back out the door and rode off again.

A few hours later, he was back. I thought about apologizing and waited for him to come into the office, but he was still sitting on his bike. He took off his helmet, and a crowd of people from other offices had gathered around him. Puzzled, I stepped outside and gasped. The hair on both sides of his head was shaved clean off. His gray-straked Mohawk spiked like a teenager's rebellion.

"I decided to get a Mohawk," he said with a feral grin. "I've always wanted one."

His audience was amused, but I wasn't. "You're supposed to be a businessman. You look ridiculous. How can anyone take you seriously when you look like an old fool?"

"Why do you have to be so negative?" he mumbled.

"I'm not negative," I said defensively. I strode back into the office, slamming the door behind me. Michael was always accusing me of something. Once, he called me frigid. His words stung, but I knew that wasn't true. I remembered the one time I had sought comfort elsewhere. A stab of guilt washed over me with the memory of my infidelity when we first moved to Georgia. Michael had convinced me I was sexually stunted until I met Austin. The affair was brief. He wanted me to leave Michael. I had to put an end to it or lose my family. Over the years, I often wondered how my life would have been if I had made a different choice.

My marriage continued to circle the drain, but I didn't know how to fix it or if I wanted to. It was easier to ignore our problems than to deal with Michael's twisted expression of loathing and caustic remarks.

Even when he berated me in front of a client, the grit I needed to protect myself wasn't there.

One afternoon, a client came to inspect her exhibit.

"Florence, please, can you do something about Michael's appearance? The convention is in one week, and I can't have, I mean, it's imperative that..."

"I'll see what I can do," I said, "but I can't promise anything."

I had hoped someone would have the nerve to tell him how stupid his hair looked, but it fell to me.

"You have to get rid of that Mohawk before the show next week."

"Everyone likes it except you!"

"No one does, but they're not going to tell you. You'll lose all your clients if you don't."

Frustrated, I went to bed early, waking up after a few hours with my mind racing. I reached for a bottle of sleeping aid.

In the morning, the smell of bacon drifted upstairs. Feeling dizzy from the sleep aid, I went down to find Michael sitting at the table, wolfing down his eggs. He loved breakfast. It was his favorite meal. I started to hate the sound of the word — breakfast.

"How's everything going with the business?" I asked.

"It's fine. Why?"

"Don't I have a right to ask?"

"Sure, but I *am* the business," he said.

"Why do you keep saying that?"

"I do all the work."

"Who do you think takes care of the payroll, insurance, schedules, and taxes? I helped you start that business. I even thought up the name of the company."

His mouth tightened. "Without me, there is no business." His voice sounded throaty.

"That's not fair. My contribution is just as valuable."

"It's not the same. If you didn't do the books, the business would survive, but if I don't work, the business will cease to exist."

"That's ridiculous!" Michael had a way of making me feel as trivial as a hiccup.

I pushed my chair away from the table to put the dishes in the sink while he poured himself a cup of coffee and took an annoying slurp.

"I may have a solution. My friend John has a shop only five miles from here. We're talking about merging."

"Partnerships are never a good idea," I said. "That was the first thing I learned in business class."

"John's a good salesman. He can keep the work and the money flowing. He'll take care of the office while I manage the show floor."

"What about me? Where do I fit into all this?"

"You said you were overworked. You can travel more. You can spend more time in Florida."

The idea was tempting. After sixteen years of payroll, insurance, and taxes, I'd lost my motivation.

"You'll still own half of my half," he said, his gaze shifting. "I would never hurt you."

Reluctantly, I allowed Michael to move the exhibits, inventory, and tools from the shop to his friend's shop. I still hadn't put two and two together.

Chapter 33 | Mary Jane

Persistent rain fell for three days straight. It would have been a gloomy week, except that Michael was on his business trip to Florida. I welcomed the stillness of the house, but there was an empty feeling in the pit of my stomach. I lingered over my cup of coffee, rummaged through the bedroom closet, and pulled out my sneakers. The only thing that has given me pleasure lately has been going to the gym. After battling with the weights, I mounted the stationary bike and frantically pedaled as if I could outrun the gloom in my life.

The ups and downs of running a business damaged our relationship. I'd thought about divorce occasionally, but hadn't wanted to uproot the children when they were young. Now, I had no more excuses.

The idea of change crushed my chest and squeezed the air from my lungs. I closed my eyes and pedaled faster, going nowhere, letting the machine's inertia propel my limp limbs in circles.

After I worked out, I was still feeling restless. I needed something to lift my mood, so I stopped by

Home Depot and browsed through the paint swatches. They seemed to glow under the display's fluorescent lights. A sample with a warm peachy hue caught my eye. I needed something bright and cheery.

With the paint can in one hand, I turned the key with the other. The front door swung open with the help of my foot, and a pungent smell of mildew filled my nostrils. I knew the rain had leaked into the sunken living room. After throwing towels down to soak up the water, I called Michael.

"What is it?" he asked.

"We have a flood in the house. The carpet is soaking wet. We'll need to rip it out."

"Don't exaggerate, Florence."

"The forecast calls for more rain, and the carpet's already smelling like mildew."

"I'll fix it when I get home."

"If you had fixed the problem in the first place, the water wouldn't have come in," I retorted.

He hung up, or maybe I did. Grabbing a shovel from the toolshed, I went outside and found the spot where the water had seeped into the living room. I stuck the shovel into a soft spot and jumped on the back of the blade until it disappeared into the earth, trying to dig a deep cavity to divert the water. Sweat ran into my eyes as I swatted the mosquitoes, looking to make me their next meal. Wiping my forehead, I took a deep breath and inhaled a gnat. Unwanted tears welled in my eyes. I glanced at the trench I had made in the dirt and debated whether my efforts would actually fix the problem. If not, I'd have to do it again.

Throwing down the shovel, I went back into the house and took a long, hot shower, letting the water flow over me.

I skipped dinner and poured myself a glass of wine, then another, feeling its effect. The dishwasher finished its cycle. Dishes rattled, and glasses clinked as I carelessly unloaded them and stacked them in the cabinets. I didn't know why, but I took out my frustrations on the utensils and threw the silverware into the drawer without organizing the forks and spoons. It was easier to slam a cabinet or break a dish than to confront the people in my life who made me angry.

When I finished, it was getting dark outside. I filled a bowl with ice cream and climbed into bed to watch television. I turned off the light and stared into the darkness until I floated into an uneasy slumber.

In the morning, the phone woke me up. It was Annmarie.

"Mom, I need you."

"What's wrong?"

"Cody and I are fighting again. Can I come home?"

"Of course. Let me get dressed, and I'll pick you up."

"No, I want to wait until he goes to work. Pick me up in an hour."

On top of everything I had to deal with, now my daughter's life was spiraling out of control.

She was already in front of her apartment when I pulled up, baby in one arm and a suitcase in the other.

"Are you all right?" I asked as she buckled my granddaughter in the back seat.

"No, I'm worried. Jason's threatening to take the baby if I leave."

"He can't do that!"

"I don't know. Things can get very ugly in a divorce."

When we arrived back at the house, a strange expression came over her face. "Where's Daddy?"

"I don't know, probably riding his motorcycle all over the country. Why?"

"I have to call Jason," she said and jumped out of the car, leaving me to get the baby.

"What's wrong?" I asked.

"Hold on!" Annmarie waved me off as she whispered into the phone.

"Are you going to tell me what's going on?" I asked when she hung up.

"He knows!"

"Who knows?" I asked. "Knows what?"

"My husband! He knows and could use it to take my daughter away from me."

I was tired of the puzzle, but sensed something terrible was about to happen. We pulled into the driveway.

"I'll show you," she said, jumping out of the car.

I followed her into the warehouse. My heart pounded so hard that I felt dizzy.

"You're scaring me," I said.

"You should be scared. You're not going to like this."

She continued to the back wall until we stood before a slat wall panel with tools hanging from the hooks.

"Help me move these tools," she said.

We began taking down rakes and shovels until they lay across the floor.

"Push that side and slide the panel toward me," Annmarie instructed.

As I pushed, the panel opened, bright light sliced into my retinas, and the loud swish of a fan invaded my ears. The pungent smell was familiar. I couldn't believe my eyes. There were over ten plants, some four feet high and two feet wide.

"Pot?" I stood there in disbelief.

"Daddy's been selling it, and my husband knows."

There were also grow lights and a ventilation system. "No wonder my electric bill is so high," I muttered.

"I wanted to tell you, but I knew you and Dad were having problems. I didn't want to make it worse."

"Wow!" Jason said, coming up behind us. I didn't hear his car pull up.

"We have to get rid of it," Annmarie pleaded.

"How?" I asked, frozen by the enormity of the situation.

Jason, level-headed as always, took charge. "I'll dig a ditch in the yard. We'll burn them."

"Burn? What about the smell?"

"We'll have to make sure the fire is hot so it goes up fast." He grabbed a shovel. "Annmarie, you start taking the plants out." He turned to me. "Mom, you go upstairs on the balcony and keep watch. Yell if you see any cars coming up the block."

"Cars?"

"Yeah, in case someone calls the police."

I took my granddaughter to the balcony, expecting a police cruiser to head straight toward my house any minute. So many things were going through my mind. I couldn't prioritize their importance.

I knew Michael did. He had smoked pot since Vietnam. However, smoking and selling were two different things. It suddenly dawned on me how he could afford so many motorcycles.

As the shock wore off, things began to make sense. *So that's why Michael didn't want me in the warehouse.*

Soon, the smell of burning pot plants drifted to the front of the house. I ran to the yard with my granddaughter in tow.

Jason and Annmarie poked at the plants in the fire with a stick, ensuring the flames consumed every lush, green stem. The three of us stood around the pit as if it were a campfire.

"It's not finished yet," Annmarie said. "We have to disassemble the lights and fans. Then, bleach the floors to get rid of any remaining residue."

"Make sure this fire doesn't go out, Mom," Jason said. "And watch for planes!"

"Hurry!" I said as the waft of smoke soared up to the sky. I poked the flames while my granddaughter ran around the yard.

"Stay away from the smoke," I cautioned, worried she might inhale it.

Anger consumed me as I thought about the implications. *Michael could have been arrested—I could have been arrested.* Pot, beer, and motorcycles were his life, not mine! Still, no one would believe I didn't know what he was doing right under my nose.

When everything was clean, Jason called Michael. I was glad I didn't have to deal with it. I didn't want to hear Michael's explanations. Years of experience told me he'd blow it off.

The pot was gone, but so was my trust, and I no longer felt safe in my home.

It was still dark outside when Michael returned from his business trip. He never called to let me know he was on his way. Either he didn't want to disturb me, or he didn't want me to know he was home. When he entered the warehouse, I shrugged and went back to bed.

In the morning, I went downstairs to find him in the kitchen. He had a strange look on his face. I thought he would complain about his marijuana farm going up in smoke, but he threw me off the track.

"I put a deposit down on a townhouse."

"What?" I shook the sleep from my eyes.

"You always said you wanted to live in Florida," he said, slapping a color brochure on the counter.

"I thought you said we couldn't afford a townhouse?"

"It's on protected land, right on the Intracoastal Waterway. This development is expected to double in value by the time it is completed. We could sell this house and retire. It's only an hour and a half from your mother."

I thumbed through the brochure. The prospective homes had Tuscan-style roofs and beautiful shuttered windows.

"It's nice, but... the housing market may go down. I'm not sure this is a good time to buy another property."

"Why do you always have to be so negative?"

"I'm not negative. I'm realistic."

"Isn't this what you wanted?"

What I wanted was a divorce!

Tempted by the beautiful landscape and the pool, I ignored my inner voice and disregarded the signs of a looming recession.

Maybe it was time for a change. Who knows, maybe we can get a grip on our slippery marriage.

Carrots and sticks! If I were a good girl, I would get a reward. Michael didn't need the stick. All he had to do was dangle the carrot.

Chapter 34 | No Rights

When we started our company, I debated whether I should make two separate paychecks for him and me. I didn't see the need for extra paperwork. We filed a joint tax return. I wrote a paycheck in Michael's name, deducting Social Security and Medicare.

Every week, I wrote out the paycheck. As the money in our business account dwindled, I shoved it to the back of my mind to deal with later.

"Stop withdrawing money from the account," Michael said. "John is getting upset."

"I need money to pay the bills."

"I'll talk to John today."

"Now, we have to get *his* permission?"

"Do you want the money or not?"

"Who exactly is this John Hamilton, anyway?"

Suddenly, I remembered a letter we received from the IRS.

"Didn't he work for us two years ago?"

"Yes, why?"

"Last April, the IRS inquired if he still worked for us."

"What did you say?"

"I told them no, but I wasn't aware you were planning to merge our business with his. Your friend owes the government back taxes."

"I'm sure he's taken care of it."

"Does John have access to our money?"

"Yes, he's on the account."

"That's not legal! John is not an officer of the company."

"Calm down. You're overreacting, as usual."

"No, I'm not. I'm the chief financial officer. That makes me liable."

"We have to do it this way until we establish the company. We don't have a federal tax ID number yet."

"You can't run another business on our tax number. It's not right, and I don't like it."

"You don't like anything! Stop complaining. You have less work now."

"I need money."

"I'm going out of town on business," he said. "You'll have to wait until I get back."

"I can't wait that long. The mortgage is due."

Michael took one last sip of his coffee and put the cup in the sink. "I'll take care of it!"

Later that afternoon, I found an envelope taped to the front door containing a check. Michael had left for a job in Miami.

In the past, I loved those trips. We'd stay at a pricey hotel, which the client had paid for, and while he was working, I would enjoy the local tourist sites or go shopping. I recalled our last trip together. Michael had insisted on taking his motorcycle along in the back of the truck. When we checked into the hotel, he didn't think it was safe and wheeled the greasy vehicle into the room through the sliding glass door that faced the parking lot.

"I can't believe you're doing this! It'll ruin the carpet, and it smells like gasoline."

Michael grabbed a comforter and tossed it over the bike. "There. Now you can't smell it."

That was our last trip together. Michael had sucked all the joy out of traveling with him.

My life didn't seem so bad when I had the house to myself. At least he left me some money. I opened the envelope and stared at the check. There was the familiar logo—the one I had designed —but the address was different, and John's name was on it.

The irony left me bewildered! John wrote me a check from my own business. Furious, I paced around the kitchen.

Anger boiled up inside me, and I picked up the phone. The fear was physical, like a fist squeezing the blood out of my heart. Michael had found a way to cut me out of our business. I didn't want to talk to him, but I had to.

"What's going on with *our* business?" I demanded.

"Stop yelling, or I'll hang up on you," he warned.

"I'm not yelling. I'm asking. When did you change the address?"

"What are you babbling about now? I'm in the middle of a job. Can we talk about this when I get home?"

"No!" I shrieked. "I want to talk about it *now*. How dare you give your friend the authority to dole out money to me from our business? That's our company name—at *his* address. I could blow the top off this whole deal."

The phone went dead. Michael hung up.

Chapter 35 | Betrayed

My breath hitched at the sound of Michael's motorcycle pulling into the driveway. I lay in bed, staring at the ceiling, and strained to hear the front door open, but the drone of the air conditioner eclipsed all other sounds. *Please don't come inside*, I thought.

After our last argument, we'd avoided each other. Michael moved his stuff into the warehouse and started sleeping in the flat above the shop.

As I was falling asleep, Michael's footsteps clambered up the stairs.

Oh, no, I thought. He's coming back to our bedroom. I pulled the covers tight around me and closed my eyes. Breathing steadily through my nose, I stayed very still.

Michael yanked back the sheets and lay down next to me. I moved in small increments to the edge of the bed.

In the morning, the smell of freshly brewed coffee drifted upstairs, nudging me out of bed and into the kitchen.

Michael stood in front of the counter, holding a cup of coffee and staring blankly.

"Good morning," he said.

"Morning," I replied, and poured myself a cup.

The usual tension after an argument hung heavy in the air.

Michael sat on one of the stools at the breakfast nook, his gaze on the steam from his coffee.

"You were right. I should never have merged the business with John. He's been screwing me over all this time."

"It's a little late to realize that now!"

"Is that all you have to say?"

"No." My breath quickened. "I want a divorce."

"You always want a divorce."

"This time, I mean it!"

"We'd have to sell the house," he taunted with a jab at my weak spot.

I stared out of the window into the yard. My garden was my pride and joy. I had landscaped flowering plants, moving them around to find the perfect place for them to thrive — gardenias, azaleas, forsythias, hostas, and a variety of fruit trees. I even cultivated honeysuckle. It grew fast and soon crawled up the hillside, covering it with sweet-smelling white flowers. Every May, their scent drifted into the house.

The blossoms on my cherry tree were in bloom, but this year, their color wasn't as vibrant as in past years. The essence of the tree had shifted. I could feel it slipping away, along with my own.

It's funny how little things can keep you stuck in a bad relationship. Even though the house was unfinished and in disrepair, it was hard to let go of the dream.

"Did you hear me?" Michael asked. "If we get divorced, we'll have to sell the house."

"Fine. We'll sell the house and split the proceeds equally, but I also want my share of the business. I'm entitled to fifty percent."

Michael folded his arms. "The company no longer exists, so technically, you own fifty-one percent of nothing."

Feeling like I had been sucker-punched, I tried to comprehend what he was saying. Michael watched me unravel.

"That's ridiculous," I said. "We started that exhibit company together!"

My heart thumped wildly, and my temperature rose as I paced the floor. A surge rippled up my spine to my head, devouring me like Joan of Arc in a blaze of fire.

"You stole the business right out from under me! I hate you!" The words gushed out of my mouth before I could stop them. The release was cleansing, but there was no way to take it back.

He threw his coffee cup in the sink and walked out of the house, leaving me alone to pick up the shattered pieces of my life.

The sound of his motorcycle faded away. I leaned against the counter for support. Tears streaming down my face, as I fell to the floor.

Marriage was supposed to be the answer to all my problems—a simple, easy life. I thought that marriage could shield me from the pressures of society. I gave in to my desire for security and followed in my mother's footsteps. I chose to be a housewife over having a career. The lifestyle seemed safer and more predictable.

But in reality, it was just a place to hide. For most of my married life, I hid behind the invisible walls of the housewife role, clinging to the belief that it would keep me safe. Instead of pursuing a career when I graduated from high school, I took what I thought was the safe route. Now, there was nothing left to shield me.

Then I remembered the business card my friend Jesse had given me—a divorce lawyer's card. He was a refined, good old Southern boy who'd taken over the reins of his father's law practice. I'd saved the card just in case. Now worn and faded, it was barely legible, but the phone number was still clear. I called and made an appointment.

Michael and I once agreed that if things ended between us, we would keep lawyers out of it. But he played dirty, and I couldn't fight him alone.

Chapter 36 | Shoot for the Stars

Michael and I had talked about divorce a million times, but somehow, I never believed it would actually happen. Love is a fragile thing. It can end as suddenly as it began, often with nothing more than a few cruel words. *Is it right to feel a sense of relief that it's over? He was my husband. I must have loved him once.*

I sat in the lawyer's parking lot, blinded by tears, trying to pull myself together. Everything was collapsing so fast. Questions swirled in my mind. *How will we divide a lifetime of accumulated stuff? Where would I live? How would I survive without the business income?*

Brushing my hair back, I wiped the smeared mascara from beneath my eyes with my fingers and took a deep breath.

Inside, the receptionist looked up from her computer and took in my tear-streaked face.

"Bless your heart," she said in a sweet Southern accent. Rising from her desk, she smoothed her pencil skirt, then gave me a hug. "Don't worry. Mr. Davis is a good lawyer — top of the heap. He'll take good care of you." She smiled gently. "Have a seat. I'll let him know you're here."

She picked up the phone and whispered into the receiver.

"Mr. Davis will be with you shortly," she said when she hung up. "You can wait in his office."

She led me down a narrow hallway. "Would you like some coffee or water?"

"No, thank you."

"If you need anything, come to the front and get me!" she said and left.

I sank into a comfortable chair in front of a mahogany desk. The scent of old leather surrounded me, and the soft lighting offered unexpected comfort. I wondered if it was intentional—an atmosphere designed to soothe anxious clients.

Mr. Davis stepped into the room, tall and composed, his silver-streaked hair swept neatly to the side. He carried himself with quiet composure—his gray Brooks Brothers suit perfectly pressed, his presence calm but commanding. He reached out to shake my hand.

"I need help," I whispered, the words catching in my throat before dissolving into sobs.

He grabbed a box of tissues from his desk and handed me one.

"Take a deep breath," he said softly. "Everything is going to be fine, I promise."

Clasping my hands nervously in my lap, I told him everything—how Michael had emptied the business account and erased me from everything we built together," I said in disbelief. "He just cut me out. Isn't that illegal?"

Mr. Davis leaned back in his chair and chewed thoughtfully on the end of his unlit pipe.

"You could fight for half," he said slowly. "But he's already drained the assets. There's not much left to fight *for*."

Despair washed over me. "So, Michael gets away with it? He steals everything, and that's it? I'm just …left with nothing?"

"There is another way," he said after a pause. "Alimony."

"People still get that?"

He smiled reassuringly. "You were married a long time. That counts for something. You're entitled to a settlement."

I straightened a little. "I don't want handouts. I just want what's mine—half the business profits."

"I hear you," he said, nodding slowly. "But going after the business means opening the door for him to claim bankruptcy. He could walk away scot-free, and you'd be left empty-handed. I'd feel better calling it alimony. We'll ask for that—*and* the house."

I stared at him, stunned. "The house?"

He opened his desk drawer and pulled out a stack of forms. "Let's shoot for the stars," he said with a wink. "We'll draft an agreement that gives you the stability you deserve. Michael doesn't have to like it— but that doesn't mean we won't fight for it."

I exhaled the breath I hadn't realized I'd been holding. For the first time in weeks, I felt something other than panic — relief, maybe even a little strength.

As I stepped out of his office into the sunlight, my shoulders lighter, I felt it — vindication. And the first glimmer of something that felt like hope.

Chapter 37 | Dark Sky

Michael's motorcycle rumbled into the driveway, then fell silent as he disappeared into his lair. I followed with the divorce agreement and a pen.

"I went to see a lawyer today," I said in a steady voice.

He looked up briefly from wiping down his bike, then tossed the rag aside with a flick of his wrist.

I handed him the preliminary divorce settlement and tried to read his expression.

"You don't actually think I'm going to sign this, do you?" he scoffed, flinging the pages into the air. "It's my house, too."

I bent down to retrieve the documents and stood my ground. "If you want half the house, I want half of the business," I said firmly. "I'm entitled to it. You pulled money from the house to keep it running. I didn't want to, but you pressured me into it. I had no choice. Financial abuse — that's what it is. You stole my equity."

"Fine," he snapped. "Take the goddamned house, but the business is mine!" He straddled his motorcycle, resentment in his eyes. He scribbled his name across the bottom of the agreement and kick-started the engine. The thunderous sound pierced my ears.

"Let me know the court date," he said before squealing out of the driveway.

On the day of the hearing, I stood outside the courthouse, waiting for Mr. Davis. Strangers passed with brisk, purposeful strides. At last, he arrived and briefed me on the procedure that was about to take place. We entered the courtroom and were seated on the right side. I kept my eyes locked on the double doors, half-hoping Michael wouldn't show.

After reading the complaint, the judge looked up. "Is Mr. Corrigan present?"

"Yes, Your Honor," Michael said, rising.

He was sitting at the back, and I hadn't seen him slip in through the double doors. Dressed in a rumpled, ill-fitting black suit, he slipped into the front row and glared at me.

"Did you sign this agreement?"

"Yes, Your Honor."

"You agree to give your wife the house and monthly alimony?"

"Yes, Your Honor."

"Do you have legal representation?"

"No, Your Honor."

"Do you require one?"

"No, Your Honor."

"Very well. Let's proceed."

Fifteen minutes. That's all it took to dissolve thirty years of marriage and take back my maiden name—St. John. Mr. Davis submitted a quitclaim deed for the house. Before the proceedings ended, Michael was gone just as abruptly as he had arrived.

"Congratulations," Mr. Davis said, shaking my hand.

"Thank you," I mumbled, but I didn't feel triumphant.

When I pulled up the driveway, reality crashed in like a wave. The house loomed before me, with its unfinished garage and missing siding. All I had was the house--and my freedom. But if you cage an animal long enough, it forgets not only what freedom feels like but what to do with it once it's finally free.

"Shoot for the stars," my lawyer had said, but as I looked up into the night sky, all I could see was darkness.

Chapter 38 | Hawthorne Yellow

My heart felt heavy as I checked the mailbox and slowly made my way up the driveway. Unlocking the front door, I half-expected to see Michael at the kitchen table, sipping his coffee like always. But, of course, he wasn't there. It wasn't supposed to turn out this way. I hadn't planned on being alone.

Two weeks had passed since the divorce. The silence in the house pressed against me—every room was too quiet, too still. After all the years I'd spent trying to free myself from him, I hadn't expected the loneliness to hit so hard. But there it was. I kicked off my shoes and poured a glass of wine, hoping it would dull the ache. Something made me wander into the warehouse—curiosity, or maybe just the need to take control of my space. The shop was stripped bare, except for beer cans, oil buckets, crumpled papers, and trash. Electrical cords dangled in a messy web from the ceiling, knotted between light fixtures and power strips. I followed an orange extension cord snaking along the ground to the back of the house, where it was plugged into an outdoor outlet Michael had recklessly rigged himself. *So that's why the breaker kept tripping,* I thought. I'd spent the past year breaking circuits whenever I turned on the vacuum or the blow dryer. The computer would suddenly shut off, and I'd find myself resetting clocks like some kind of weary timekeeper.

I shuffled through the mail, my mind still adjusting to divorce. We hadn't spoken since it was finalized. Michael ignored my calls. I thought, even if we parted, we'd manage civility—for our children if nothing else. But he treated me like a stranger now. Like I'd stopped being a person the moment I stopped being his wife.

Maybe he was shocked at how fast our marriage unraveled. For me, the split had been a slow, agonizing crawl. But I still held out hope we could be civil. I picked up the phone and called my daughter.

"Have you seen your father?" I asked. "I haven't heard from him."

"What do you expect? You divorced him."

"I expect him to act like an adult. He's not the victim here," I said, trying to hold back the sting in my voice.

"I don't want to take sides, Mom."

"I'm not trying to make you take sides. Just tell me where he's staying."

She sighed. "I think he's living in the warehouse."

"I thought he merged the business into his friend John's warehouse."

"He did, but Dad found out that John was skimming money, so he rented a new shop. He had to break into his friend's place in the middle of the night to get his stuff out."

"It doesn't surprise me. I knew that partnership would fall apart."

"Well, don't say anything if you see him. He'll know I told you."

"Don't worry. I won't."

I hung up and stared out the window. Michael had been so afraid I'd steal the business that he handed the reins to someone who actually did.

Three weeks later, Michael stormed into the house like a ghost from the past. He looked... older... grayer. His clothes were wrinkled and hung on him like they didn't quite belong.

"Where have you been?" I asked.

"I don't have to answer to you," he said, his voice flat. "We're divorced."

I swallowed hard. The lump in my throat was impossible to ignore. The doctor called it anxiety, but that didn't begin to explain the ache.

He grabbed a few of his things, and I followed him out to his truck.

"Why are you being like this? We're still a family."

"You destroyed our family!"

"I had no choice. You stole half the company. Do you think any of this makes me happy?"

"You're never happy," he muttered. "Even the kids can't stand your negativity."

Ouch!

When he drove off, I went back into the house. The answering machine light was blinking. I wondered if I should go back to Long Island. It was a reflex. The truth was, I couldn't afford to live in New York. Besides, I wanted to live in Florida. That's where my mother was now. I didn't belong in Georgia. I knew that twenty-six years ago. The only thing that held me was the house.

I braced myself and pressed play on the answering machine.

"This is Joe Antonelli from Century Builders in Florida. Just calling to let you know the final inspection of your townhouse is complete. You're good to move in."

The townhouse! That was the carrot Michael had dangled in front of me, hoping it would fix everything. It wasn't enough. Or maybe it just came too late. Even if it had only existed in theory, that dream was still alive for me.

According to the divorce agreement, Michael had to keep paying the mortgage on the Florida townhouse until it was sold—and that wouldn't be anytime soon. With the market still soft, it may take some time. For now, Michael was stuck with the payment.

Maybe I can move to Florida. I was ready to let go of Georgia and take a chance on somewhere new. But I first had to sell the house. I called a local real estate office to start the process.

When Bob Morrissey showed up to take listing photos, I was hopeful—until we started walking through the house.

"I'll be honest," he said. "The market's soft, and this place needs work."

"I have to sell," I said urgently. I'm moving to Florida. Maybe we can list it as a handyman special."

"It could use a fresh coat of paint," he said gently.

"I can handle that."

"Okay. I'll put up the listing, and we'll hope for the best."

As soon as he left, I went to Home Depot for paint and supplies. I chose Hawthorne Yellow—a cheerful color I saw on some home makeover show. But once it was on the wall, I hated it. Forty-five dollars wasted, and now I had to do it all over again.

Paint cans and brushes lay on the tarp, and my mood spiraled into despair. Then I remembered the swatch I'd picked out for the Florida townhouse. It was still tucked in my purse. Textured paint—perfect for covering the cracks and dings in the walls. I took it to Home Depot, but no one had a clue what I was talking about. Blank stares. Shrugs.

Chapter 39 | For Rent

The next morning, I looked at the back of the swatch. Sherwin-Williams. Of course. A quick search told me there was one just five miles away. I waited in the parking lot until the *Open* sign lit up. Inside, I handed the sample to the clerk.

"I hope you can help," I said. "No one else knows how to do this."

"Oh yeah, I've seen this technique," he said. "It's called *Knockout*. There's a guy who does this around here—comes in all the time."

"Do you have his number?"

"Hey, Lou!" he shouted into the back. "What's the name of that texture guy?"

Lou emerged from the stockroom. "We've got his flyer around here somewhere." He rummaged under the counter. "Here it is."

I stared at the flyer. "Yes! That's it," I said, smiling.

"Not many people ask for this style here. It's big in Florida," Lou said. "His name's Dale."

"Thank you so much," I said, clutching the flyer like it was gold.

Before I even left the parking lot, I called the number.

"Hi, is this Dale?"

"Yes, ma'am. How can I help you?" His voice had a soft Southern lilt.

"I need an estimate for textured painting."

"I'm sorry. I'm all booked this month."

"Please. I've been everywhere. You're the only one who knows how to do this."

He paused. "Well... I might be able to swing by and take a look. I have four jobs ahead of you. Could you please provide your address? I'll come by this afternoon."

"Thank you," I said. Hope surging through me again, I turned the car toward home.

Before Dale even knocked, I swung the front door open. He jumped back like he'd seen a ghost, clutching his chest.

"Jesus, lady! You just about scared the life outta me."

"Sorry," I said, trying to steady my nerves. "I guess I'm a little on edge."

Dale spat a dark stream of tobacco juice into the grass and wiped his mouth.

Gross!

"Name's Dale," he said, offering his hand. "You must be Florence."

"That's me. Come on in. I'll show you around."

He slipped off his flip-flops, left them by the door, and followed me down the hallway, his eyes sweeping over the walls.

"I tried to paint," I said. "Didn't exactly go according to plan."

He gave a low whistle. "Sure didn't. But I've seen worse," he added with a grin.

Dale moved slowly through each room, tapping on the walls and running a finger over the cracks in the plaster. "These I can fix. Paint'll help. But you've got more going on here. Trim's in rough shape, and you're missing pieces in a few spots."

"I know. It's just—" I hesitated.

"And those ceilings," he cut in. "Gotta be painted too."

I folded my arms. "I can't afford to do it all."

He shrugged. "Tell you what—I'll give you a flat price. One deal, everything covered. When I'm done, this place'll look brand new. Scout's honor."

I didn't know Dale from Adam, but something about him—maybe his easy smile—made me believe he could pull it off. Still, the number he quoted would take a bite out of my emergency fund. A big one.

When I walked him out, my eyes caught the bumper stickers on his truck. *Vegetables are not food! They're what food eats.* And right below it, *"Ditch the Bitch, Let's Go Hunting."*

Charming.

Dale noticed my expression and laughed. "Yankee, huh?"

"I'm from New York."

He winked. "I like a city woman. Maybe you and I can grab a drink sometime?"

I gave a vague smile. "We'll see," I said, not wanting to hurt his feelings.

After he drove off, I poured a glass of iced tea and stretched out in a lawn chair, letting the late afternoon sun soak into my bones. Dating hadn't crossed my mind in a long time. But Dale? He had that scruffy, Southern-boy charm you only see in old movies. Part Rhett Butler, part cowboy. Still, the chewing tobacco? That was hard to get past.

Dale worked for two weeks, and I had to admit — he delivered. The house looked alive again, full of promise. For a moment, I even considered staying. But then I remembered the Florida townhouse. And my mother. I sighed, picked up the phone, and called the realtor.

"Mr. Morrissey? Any interest in the house?"

"Oh, hey there, Florence! You're the big yellow one at the end of the cul-de-sac, right? How's it going?"

"I'm hanging in there, but I really need to sell before winter hits."

He sighed. "It's a tough market. Traditional homes just aren't moving. Realistically, we're looking at spring."

"Please — just try."

"I'll do what I can."

I hung up and called my mother. "Mom?" I cried. "I won't be able to sell my house until spring—and that's if I'm lucky. I can't do another winter here. I just can't."

"Well," she said, "why don't you rent out Jason's old room? Maybe Annmarie's too. That way, you could leave Georgia before you find a buyer."

"Rent?" I blinked. "Actually, that's not a bad idea. Both rooms have private entrances. It could work."

Wasting no time, I posted an ad on Craigslist and started boxing up everything sentimental. Then I threw out stuff I should've gotten rid of years ago and hauled it to the trash cans. It felt good. Like I was shedding old skin.

Chapter 40 | Merry-Go-Round

The first potential renter was Thomas. He was huge and had to duck to get through the doorway.

"Hi. I'm Thomas," he said, offering a quick smile. He looked around and opened the closet door.

"The fuse box is in there," I explained. "Sometimes the breaker trips, and I have to reset it, so I might need to come in once in a while. I also have a room upstairs that you're welcome to see. It's bigger and gets more light."

We climbed the exterior staircase to what used to be Annmarie's room.

Thomas loved it. I wasn't surprised—it was the sunniest part of the house—but I felt a twinge of hesitation.

"I was kind of hoping to rent this room to a woman," I said softly.

Thomas picked up on my unease. "I promise you won't regret renting to me. I work all week and go out of town every other weekend. You'll barely even know I'm here. I can pay the first and last month's rent right now."

"Okay," I said, tempted by the money up front.

He wrote me a check, and I handed it to him.

"I'll be back with my stuff next weekend."

Two days later, Justin responded to the ad. He was a college student, but he seemed responsible, so I rented him the other room.

Thomas and Justin moved in on the same day, nearly colliding as they hauled in boxes and bags. I watched from the window, then retreated to my room. Later that night, lying in bed, I listened to the unfamiliar sounds of strangers settling into my house. The walls were thin — too thin. I heard the click of Thomas's fan, the flush of the toilet from Justin's room, and the occasional thud of footsteps above.

My mind wouldn't stop spinning. I tossed and turned, finally reaching for the Tylenol PM on my nightstand. I twisted off the cap and shook two tablets into my palm. It was already 5:00 a.m. If I took them now, I'd sleep through half the day. With a sigh, I dropped the pills back into the bottle and sat up.

Within the hour, I had packed a suitcase with my summer clothes and toiletries. I loaded it into the trunk, along with some blankets, pillows, and towels. Then scooped up my cat, Riley, and locked the front door behind me.

For years, the fear of being alone had kept me tethered to Michael. But staying had been its own kind of loneliness. My life was slipping away, and I had to take the risk. It was terrifying but also exhilarating.

I headed south, the windows rolled down, a warm breeze whirring through the car. Riley sat in his carrier on the back seat, occasionally meowing in protest. On the passenger seat sat a small cardboard box containing the gold key to the townhouse. The gate code for the development was scrawled on the inside of the lid.

Previously, I could only sneak away to Florida for a week or two at a time. But now that I was divorced, I was finally free. Free to go where I wanted, do what I pleased, and — maybe most importantly — be whoever I wanted to be.

As the sun dropped low on the horizon, casting the world in a golden haze, I pulled into Provence Bay. I punched in the four-digit code, and the gates swung open to welcome me. I parked in the driveway and walked to the door. When the key clicked in the lock, the door opened, and the scent of fresh paint and new carpet met me. The townhouse felt untouched, waiting for me to claim it.

Mr. Johnson had told me I had until the end of the month to switch the electricity into my name, so I wandered from room to room, flipping on lights and letting the place come alive. On the kitchen table sat a small black device labeled "Garage Remote." Delighted, I rushed outside and pressed the button. Like magic, the garage door rose smoothly. I'd always wanted one in Georgia, but Michael never got around to it.

I drove the car into the garage, careful not to scrape the sides, then popped the trunk and brought in my things. As the door closed behind me, I stood in the quiet dimness of the auxiliary light and reached for the knob of the interior door.

Too tired to do much more, I spread out my blankets and pillows on the plush carpet and curled up next to Riley, already purring. Even he seemed content to be out of Georgia.

Later, unable to sleep, I opened my laptop and logged into my high school alumni page. I hadn't been popular back then, so it was surprising to see how many people remembered me.

There was a new message in my inbox. I clicked on it.

"Do you remember me? We sat next to each other in studyhall."

It was from Daniel Weaver. I had to reach far back into memory, but I saw him—a lanky boy with long blond hair, always cracking jokes.

"Yes, I do," I typed.

His reply came quickly. "When I saw your profile, I almost hit the floor. You haven't changed a bit. Still, that beautiful Italian girl with the sad brown eyes. I should've dated you back then."

"You should've…lol."

"Lol," he echoed. "How are you?"

"I recently got divorced," I admitted. "Other than that, I'm okay. I live in Georgia, but I'm trying to sell the house and move to Florida. I hired a contractor to paint the inside."

"I hate painting," he said. "Do you miss New York?"

"Yes, but I visit often. What about you? Are you still on Long Island?"

"I'm upstate now, but I'm working in Nevada at the moment."

"Doing what?"

"I run a contracting company. Right now, I'm building a retaining wall and an Olympic-sized pool for some rich lady. I'll send pics. Maybe we can meet up in Vegas!"

I laughed out loud, entertained by the suggestion. "Tempting, but I don't think I can get away."

"Then we'll have to meet next time we're both in New York. Is it okay if I contact you again?"

"I'd like that."

In the morning, I woke up feeling happy but sore. I rolled over and looked around the bare townhouse, imagining what it might look like fully furnished. I had always wanted a new bedroom set, but Michael never saw the point. He said the stores were overpriced and claimed he could build one himself, though he never did. Now, for the first time in years, I didn't have to ask for permission. I was going to buy myself a bedroom set.

I had a clear view of the Intracoastal Waterway through the living room's sliding glass doors. I imagined placing a desk there, in a peaceful spot where I could write or work on the computer and watch the boats go by. I hung artwork, too—something I never did back in Georgia. Michael always complained that the house didn't feel homey, but whenever I tried to decorate, he found fault with it. I eventually gave up, discouraged by the cracked walls and endless repairs.

In my new place, it was different. I carefully unrolled the prints I'd bought years ago in France—photographs and sketches I had stored in cardboard tubes under my bed. I placed them in bronze frames and hung them on the walls. It felt like home. Still, the divorce had left more than financial baggage. It put distance between my children and me. Annmarie wasn't speaking to me. After another painful argument, she had returned to her husband against my advice. And my son had grown distant, too. The silence from them echoed loudest of all. I found myself digging through old photo albums, pulling out pictures of them as babies. Their round, innocent faces smiled up at me, unburdened by judgment or anger. Back then, they needed me, trusted me, and looked up to me.

My mother and sister lived just an hour and a half south—Far enough for space, but close enough for comfort. We went out to lunch or lounged in my mother's living room, talking for hours. Yet, I couldn't sit still for long. My eyes wandered over her walls, noticing chipped paint and the wallpaper border I had once hung, now peeling with age.

In the past, I would have jumped into action, dragging out paint and brushes, but at fifty-five, I just didn't have it in me anymore. The fixer in me had faded. I sipped my iced tea and watched Carol scroll through her laptop.

"There's this guy who contacted me," I said suddenly. "I knew him from high school. He wants to meet up."

Carol perked up. "Have you seen a picture of him?"

"He sent one. It's kind of blurry," I said, jumping up to grab my laptop. I pulled up the email. There he was—Daniel—standing on a merry-go-round with a little girl I assumed was his daughter.

"He has nice eyes," Carol said. "What does he do?"

"He's a contractor. Right now, he's working on a house in Nevada." I smirked. "He wants me to meet him in Vegas."

Carol raised her eyebrows. "He looks like a nice guy. So what are you afraid of?"

"I'm not afraid," I said a little too quickly.

"You're single now. Start dating!"

"I hate dating. I don't even like the idea of it."

"Don't knock it until you try it! You go to the movies alone. You go out to eat alone. You even go on vacation alone."

"It's easier. I never know what to say when a man talks to me."

Carol rolled her eyes. "You need someone in your life."

"I have my computer. That's all I need."

She laughed. "You can't go out on the town with your computer."

"It's safer," I joked.

"Maybe this Daniel is the *one*."

"We'll see," I laughed, not quite ready to believe it, but not ready to rule it out either.

Chapter 41 | Six Degrees of Separation

The sun streamed through the window the next morning, warm and golden on my face. I stayed in bed a little longer than usual, staring at the ceiling and listening to Riley purr at my feet.

Michael didn't want to talk to me anymore—not that I was surprised. I had warned him, time and again, that I couldn't keep living the way we were. For years, I begged him to start fresh somewhere else, to move out of Georgia. All he ever wanted was to smoke pot, ride his motorcycle, and pretend nothing needed fixing. Eventually, I stopped asking.

I slipped into my swimsuit and grabbed a towel for the beach.

A warm breeze kissed my cheek. My bare feet sank into the soft pink sand scattered with tiny white shells that gleamed in the sun. The ocean sighed gently beside me, and for a moment, everything—every burden, every bruise—melted away. I breathed in the salty air and let Florida seduce me with its lulling rhythm. I was finally beginning to believe I could start over.

Georgia flickered in the back of my mind, but I pushed the thought aside like a bad dream. I wasn't ready to face that house — or the ghosts I'd left inside it. For once, I let myself be happy. My cell phone buzzed with a Georgia area code. I hesitated before answering.

"Hi, this is Justin. Sorry to bother you, but I've got a problem," he said, his voice tight with frustration.

"What's wrong?" I asked, already bracing myself.

"It's the guy upstairs. He leaves the TV blaring all night. I haven't slept in three days. I tried asking him nicely — he told me to go to hell."

My stomach dropped. "I'm sorry. Maybe if you talk to him again —"

"I'm done, Florence. I can't live like this. I'm moving out. I'll text you an address to send the deposit."

The call ended before I could find the right words. I stared at the screen, numb. Without Justin's rent, I couldn't cover the mortgage. I tried calling Thomas, but he didn't answer, and it went straight to voicemail.

My cell rang again. Bob from Valley View Realty. My heart stuttered with fragile hope. Maybe — just maybe — he had good news.

"Hi, Bob. Did you find a buyer?"

There was a beat of silence too long to be hopeful.

"Florence, we've got a big problem."

The knot in my stomach cinched tighter. "Problem?"

"I took a client to the house this morning. I knocked on the upstairs door and explained it was a showing. The tenant told me to leave, or he'd beat the crap out of me."

I closed my eyes. "Oh my God. Do you want me to call him?"

"It's too late. The client left. And Florence, I can't show the house again until that tenant's gone. It's not safe. I'm sorry."

The line went dead. Disappointment surged through me. My dream of moving forward had snapped like a brittle branch. There was only one thing left to do.

I drafted a notice for Thomas to vacate and sent it. He had thirty days, but I prayed he'd go sooner. I remained in Florida as long as I could, clinging to denial. I'd spent a lifetime avoiding conflict—biting my tongue to keep the peace. But not this time.

This time, I would drive straight into the storm. I would face Thomas in Georgia—the one place I swore I'd never return to.

Chapter 42 | Evicted

It was well past midnight when I pulled into the driveway of my house in Georgia. A pale light flickered in the upstairs window—I figured it was coming from Thomas's television. I stayed in the car for a moment, gathering my courage. Then I popped the trunk. Although my suitcase had wheels, I lifted it by the handle, not wanting to make a sound. Keys in hand, I crept toward the front door.

The porch light clicked on at the first hint of motion, and I froze.

My heart pounded as I fumbled for the keyhole. I slipped inside and quickly locked the deadbolt behind me. The house was quiet, aside from the low hum of Thomas's TV upstairs.

I didn't turn on any lights. Instead, I poured a glass of water from the kitchen faucet and tiptoed up the stairs. As I set the glass on my nightstand, the pictures on the wall suddenly rattled.

"I'm not going anywhere!" Thomas shouted, followed by a loud bang against the wall.

Only a hallway and a locked door separated his room from mine.

I crept downstairs, opened the kitchen drawer, and pulled out a knife. Then I sat in the hallway, every muscle in my body tense. The knife trembled in my hand as I listened to the creak of floorboards. Thomas was pacing from room to room, muttering, slamming things.

I didn't move. I just waited, my breath shallow. *Tomorrow*, I thought. *I'll evict him tomorrow.*

Eventually, my exhaustion overwhelmed the fear. On my hands and knees, I crawled back to my bedroom and placed the knife beside the glass of water. Sleep came in restless waves.

In the middle of the night, I woke up and reached for the glass of water on my nightstand. It wasn't there! After a moment, I realized I was in Georgia. My water was on the nightstand in Florida. I didn't know where I was half the time. It unnerved me.

In the morning, I slipped out and drove to the courthouse. I circled the parking lot three times, searching for a spot. A young couple walked hand in hand toward their car, laughing softly. They stopped to kiss, and a sudden ache bloomed in my chest. *Would I ever have that kind of happiness?* I had spent so many years waiting for change, for love, for something better. I felt like an outsider pressing my nose to the glass of a life I had once imagined for myself. A car horn jolted me back to reality. I pulled forward and finally found a parking spot. Inside, the security line crawled. When it was finally my turn, the wire in my bra set off the metal detector.

"Arms out," the guard instructed as he waved a wand over me.

"Where's the county clerk's office?" I asked.

"Fifth floor," he replied without looking up.

The elevator opened onto a crowded processing room. Only one window was open, and five people waited ahead of me. Finally, I stepped up to the window.

"I need to evict a tenant," I said.

The woman behind the glass handed me a clipboard. "Fill this out."

"I rented a room in my house to a man and —"

She paused and studied me. "Has he threatened you?"

"No," I said. "But I live alone, and I'm scared."

She gave me a long, assessing look. "Do you have somewhere else you can stay? A friend or family nearby?"

I shook my head. "No. There's no one."

The only time I left the house was to run to the supermarket—and even then, I made sure Thomas's old Pinto wasn't in the driveway. I peeked through the curtains. He was gone. Grabbing my purse, I rushed out and jumped into my car.

When I returned, I saw a police cruiser turning into my driveway. *Perhaps the county is serving Thomas with an eviction notice.* I pulled over to the side of the road and waited, watching the patrol car with anxiety. Ten minutes passed. Then, the cruiser pulled back onto the road, heading in my direction. I flagged it down. The officer lowered his window.

"Sorry to bother you," I began. "You were just at my house. Were you there to serve an eviction notice? I'm having a serious problem with my tenant and—" I stopped mid-sentence, my eyes drifting to the back seat. Thomas was sitting there, *smiling* at me. My jaw dropped. The officer was talking, but his voice sounded distant, as if it were underwater. I didn't hear a word. He rolled up his window and drove off.

I grabbed the phone and called the courthouse. "I need information on an eviction I filed."

"Case number?" the clerk asked.

I searched my paperwork and gave her the number.

"Please hold."

The minutes dragged, and finally, she returned. "The eviction was not filed."

"What? Why not?"

"There was a warrant out for this man. His real name is Ted Clemens."

"Ted Clemens? What was his crime?"

"I'm sorry, ma'am. I can't disclose that. He'll go before the judge in the morning. At that time, he might be jailed or released on bail."

"Bail? Does that mean he could come back here?"

"Well… yes, if that's his registered address."

"No! He *can't* come back. I'm afraid to stay here with him living in my house."

"Is there someone you could stay with for now?"

"This is *my* house! Why should I be the one to leave?"

"I understand, ma'am, but it's the law."

"What are the chances he'll make bail?"

"That depends on whether he's considered a flight risk. The judge may set it high — or deny it altogether."

I hung up and sat on the steps at the end of the hallway. My emotions were raw. My thoughts scattered.

Thomas was scheduled to appear before the judge at 2 p.m. I knew the hearing would take some time.

Gripping the cordless phone, I wandered from room to room, my eyes constantly drifting to the clock above the kitchen sink. I finally worked up the nerve to call for an update. The line was busy. I tried again. On the fifth attempt, it rang.

"I need information on a Thomas … I mean, Ted Clemens," I stammered.

"They deported Mr. Clemens to a Texas prison about an hour ago. He's been on the run since the summer."

"What — what did he do?"

"He kidnapped a college student and raped her."

"Oh my God," I whispered. "I had a rapist living under my roof!"

Chapter 43 | Past Due

I didn't think things could get any worse—until I opened the mailbox a few days later. Mixed in with the junk mail was a stark white envelope from the bank. My pulse quickened as I tore it open.

Past Due Notice: 60 Days.

I read it again. The mortgage on the Florida townhouse was two months behind. That couldn't be right, I thought. Michael always paid it by the first of the month. *Maybe it was an error. Maybe he forgot.*

My fingers trembled as I dialed his number.

"What do you want?" he said flatly.

"I just got a notice. The mortgage on the townhouse is sixty days late."

"Business is slow. I'll try to pay it next week."

Try? "That's not very reassuring."

"Is that all?"

Before I could answer, the line went dead.

I stared at the phone, shocked. *Should I call back?*

Instead, I called the number on the notice.

"This is an attempt to collect a debt. Any information obtained will be used for that purpose."

The words made my chest tighten. *A debt. Me, in default?*

A woman answered. "This is Ashley. How can I help you?"

"I need to speak to someone about my mortgage," I said, steadying my voice.

She asked for my name and account number. I gave them, then waited.

Finally, she said, "This loan is in default. Are you calling to make a payment?"

"No. My ex-husband was supposed to take care of it — Michael Corrigan."

"I see his name on the account. Do you know if this is just a temporary situation?"

"I don't know," I admitted, my throat tightening. *What if it wasn't?*

"If you're having trouble making the payments, you might qualify for a loan modification. We could lower your monthly amount."

A flicker of hope sparked in me. "Really? How do I apply?"

"I can mail the application to you."

"All right," I said, but a knot of anxiety formed in my gut. I'd need Michael's signature.

I called him back.

"What good is modifying the loan?" he said. "The place is already up for sale."

"I want to take it over."

"You can't afford it — even with a modification."

"I can if I sell the house in Georgia. I have to try. But I need your signature. The bank won't move forward without it."

"Fine. Send it. I'll fill it out when I have time."

Click.

Once again, I was left with a dial tone. A sinking weight of uncertainty pressed down on my chest.

Two weeks went by. The mortgage was still unpaid, and the bank had never received the modification application with Michael's signature.

Instead of calling, I texted him. "You said you would pay the mortgage. What happened?"

"I told you I would *try* to pay the mortgage."

"If you don't pay the loan, it'll default."

"The economy is in the toilet. 2009 isn't going to be a good year for anybody — myself included."

"They'll foreclose!" I groveled. "I need more time to sell the house in Georgia. Please!"

"I've decided I'm not going to pay the mortgage anymore. I suggest you pack up and leave."

Leave? I stared at his message in disbelief. Michael wasn't going to help me keep the townhouse. I had to do it myself. Once again, I called the mortgage company.

"This is an attempt to collect a debt. Any information obtained will be used for that purpose," the recording warned.

I hit zero and skipped the robotic message, and pleaded my case to the agent on the line. But without

Michael's signature, their hands were tied. The woman on the other end gently suggested I assume the mortgage myself. *Take over the mortgage? Can I afford that?*

What I needed was a job. Determined, I revamped my résumé and submitted dozens of online applications. When I reached the occupation field, I hesitated. I couldn't bring myself to check the box labeled 'homemaker.' It didn't capture the years I spent juggling books, raising children, and keeping a business afloat. I wasn't just a housewife—I had value.

Out of all those applications, only one agency responded, offering a commission-only sales position that required me to cover the cost of training and provide a dedicated business line.

"Some job," I muttered bitterly.

The working world had changed. No more walking into an office and shaking hands with a manager. Everything was impersonal. Sending applications felt like tossing them into space.

With my bachelor's degree in hand, it was painfully clear. Experience mattered a lot more! And without a paycheck soon, I'd lose the townhouse. Unless I could sell the house in Georgia in time.

The soft patter of rain against the window only made the silence heavier. I felt a bone-deep loneliness I hadn't expected. It caught me off guard. Hadn't I always said I wanted to be alone? No—that wasn't quite true. I didn't want to be alone. I just wanted to be left alone. There's a difference.

Unable to sleep, I crept downstairs and logged onto Facebook. A message popped up from Daniel Weaver.

"Where've you been? You didn't run off and get married, did you?"

"I haven't heard from you either," I typed back. "I was starting to think maybe you were incarcerated."

"Is it okay if I call you?"

I typed out my phone number.

"Give me ten minutes," he said.

I sat at my desk, waiting. When the phone finally rang, my breath caught in my throat.

"Heyyyy," he said, his voice smooth and confident, touched with that unmistakable New York edge. "We should've done this a long time ago."

"I still can't believe you found me after all these years," I said

"I'm into this kind of thing — tracking down people from the past."

"LMAO! Let's fly to New Orleans and meet for coffee and a beignet," he joked.

"No, let's meet in Jamaica."

"If we meet in Jamaica, we're having more than coffee."

"Fine. You make the arrangements and let me know."

"Will do!" he said — but we both knew he was teasing.

"I'm going to visit my cousins in New York next month," I said. " I booked a hotel."

"Really? I should be finished with my job by now. Maybe we could meet in the city. Call me when you get there. I'll catch a train and meet you. " We can go for that coffee."

My heart rate jumped. "Great!" I said.

I wasn't sure I was ready, but I didn't have anything to lose. And, I was single.

Before I could second-guess myself, I booked a hotel room in Manhattan.

Chapter 44 | Brooklyn Bridge

After landing at LaGuardia airport, I stood in line for the bus into the city. As I waited, my thoughts drifted back to high school. Daniel had been scrawny with messy blond hair and a mischievous smile. He wasn't my type, but he had made me laugh.

I checked into my hotel and called him. "Still coming?"

"On the train now," he said. "See you in an hour."

We agreed to meet in the hotel lounge. As I rushed down, nerves buzzing, I nearly crashed into him in the lobby.

"He-y-y!" he called out, that familiar New York accent still intact.

We hugged. Daniel was older, still handsome in that bad-boy kind of way. For a moment, we just stood there, unsure of what would come next.

"Coffee?"

"Or pizza," I said. "I know a good place under the Brooklyn Bridge."

His eyes widened. "I love pizza!"

We left the hotel and headed to the subway station. Steam rose from the grates as we walked. "Remember when you tried to kiss me under the stairwell?" he teased.

"I did not! You tried to kiss me."

We laughed, falling into an easy rhythm.

"How long were you married?" he asked.

"Thirty years."

"Wow. What happened?"

"We grew apart. I went back to school, and he started smoking pot."

"You should've married me!" He laughed.

We exited the subway station at the closest stop and walked the rest of the way. By the time we reached Grimaldis, my feet were killing me. The line was down the block. We took our place behind a group of teenagers. Daniel had them laughing in no time. He reminded me of my father—charming and magnetic. After dinner, we walked the bridge, hand-in-hand, lost in conversation.

"Let's see the Rockefeller Center tree," he said.

"It's far," I groaned, thinking about my aching feet.

When we got there, the tree was bare.

"Oh no," I said. "I forgot—they don't decorate it until after Thanksgiving."

"Bummer!" He grinned. "Let's find a bar."

The music was loud, and the bar was packed, but we managed to squeeze in. After a couple of drinks, Daniel checked his watch.

"It's after midnight. I missed the last train."

"Come back to my hotel," I offered, surprising myself.

Making our way through the hotel lobby, I began to have second thoughts. As we rode the elevator, he caught my nervous glance.

"No stress, no pressure," he said.

I swallowed hard and reminded myself that I was no longer married and wasn't doing anything wrong.

Once in the room, we opened the bottle of wine I'd bought earlier.

After two glasses, he stripped down to his boxers. They read *Control Freak* in bold letters. I laughed.

"What's so funny?" he asked.

"Nothing!"

He moved closer and kissed me. I tasted the faint trace of tobacco on his breath, but desire overpowered everything else, and we fell into bed. Wrapped in his arms, I melted into the moment. When it was over, he asked if I was okay.

"I'm more than okay," I whispered.

The clock read 2:30. I should've been asleep, but instead, I stared out the window at the New York skyline, listening to him breathe.

The horizon outside the hotel window lit up as we lay entwined in each other's arms. I turned toward Daniel and studied his face. He was undeniably still handsome.

His eyes remained closed, but he cradled my head and planted a gentle kiss on my forehead. "Do you have time to grab a cup of coffee?"

"I think so. My cousins aren't expecting me until this afternoon."

We dressed and walked across the street to a small café on the corner, where we chose a table outside.

Over coffee, Daniel took long drags on his cigarette and exhaled short puffs of smoke that encircled his head like a storm cloud.

After our coffee, we walked toward the subway station. Daniel lit another cigarette, so we stood at the top of the stairs until he finished.

The train slowed as it entered the station.

"I'll talk to you soon," he said, and gave me a quick kiss on the cheek.

As the train rolled out, I tried to keep him in my sight, but he disappeared into the crowd. I wondered if I'd ever see him again, then decided it was a one-night stand, and I was okay with that.

My cell phone chimed with an incoming text.

"Do you miss me yet? Lol."

Strangely, I did.

Chapter 45 | Rusty Nail

By 2009, the housing market had gone into freefall. Prices were plummeting across Georgia and Florida, and every week another "For Sale" sign popped up on my street. Mr. Morrissey called to say a prospective buyer had made an offer, twenty thousand dollars below the house's value. It wasn't enough to save the townhouse, so I turned it down.

"The market's sinking fast," he warned. "I can't promise you'll get a better offer."

"Is there anything I can do to make the house more appealing?"

"You might want to tackle the landscaping," he said. "It's the first thing buyers notice, and frankly, it looks like a junkyard."

"I'll take care of it this week."

The roof needed work, weeds pushed up through cracks in the driveway, and English ivy crawled up the oak tree. I yanked a vine loose—dirt flew, bark scraped off, and bits of it smacked me in the face. Inside, the circuit breakers kept tripping. The whole house felt like it was slowly falling apart, and I braced myself for whatever would go wrong next. *I should have just taken the offer.*

Fueled by a sudden burst of energy, I started cleaning out the garage. I lit the fire pit in the yard to burn the piles of wood and debris. The Georgia sun blazed overhead as I scanned the treetops. Not even a whisper of wind, so I kept feeding the flames, searching for anything that would burn. I rushed to finish trimming the hedges. Careful with my footing, I tossed the clippings onto the fire pit. Even before noon, the sun was already baking everything in sight. Sweat stung my eyes.

A sharp pain shot through my heel. I screamed and dropped to the ground, grabbing at the wooden plank that impaled my foot—a two-inch nail jutting out of it. No blood—just a small puncture, but the pain was immediate and intense.

I sat on the lawn and cried, remembering all the times I'd injured myself on tools or junk Michael had left lying around. It felt like he'd rigged the place with traps just for me.

"Lockjaw!" I gasped, trying to remember the last time I'd gotten a tetanus shot.

Once I'd pulled myself together, I limped back inside and rummaged through the medicine cabinet for an old bottle of iodine. I cleaned the wound, bandaged my foot, and sat there, seething. The pain didn't compare to the anger I felt at the mess Michael had left behind.

Homes were sitting on the market for months. Most sellers were slashing their prices and walking away with nothing.

Like a beacon cutting through the gloom or recession, another email lit up my inbox. The buyer was back. He still wanted the house—and this time, he'd made a higher offer. With the economy already in a deep recession, I knew how lucky I was to have any buyer at all.

I was leaving Georgia for good, but I couldn't go without saying goodbye to my son. I hadn't spoken to Jason since before the divorce. It had created a gap between us that I didn't know how to close. Even if I stayed, I wasn't sure how to fix what had broken. I knew he was trying to stay neutral, and I did my best to understand. Still, it hurt.

I took a deep breath and picked up the phone.

"Hi, Jason. I haven't heard from you."

"Sorry, Mom. I've been busy. Are you okay?"

"I'm fine," I said with a sigh. "But I'm selling the house. I have a buyer."

"You're selling the house?"

"I know it's your childhood home, but I'm moving to Florida."

"Dad's going to flip when he hears that. He'd probably rather see it burn to the ground."

For a moment, doubt crept in. Had I made another mistake?

"Oh well," Jason said. "You've gotta do what you've gotta do."

"I love you, Jason. Don't ever forget that."

"Okay, Mom," he chuckled. "No need to get sappy. I love you, too."

The headlines about record foreclosures and falling home prices couldn't shake my optimism. After the closing, I'd have enough money to buy the townhouse. I wanted to keep my furniture, but it didn't make sense. Storing it would cost too much. *Time for a clean start*, I thought.

Bob Morrissey met me at the title company, where I was signing the paperwork to sell the house. Some of the stress would finally lift, but it still felt bittersweet.

After initialing what felt like a hundred pages and paying off the rest of the mortgage, I'd have a little left to put in the bank. Room by room, the house emptied. All that was left were a few boxes of the things that meant the most to me. Just when I thought I was catching up, the phone rang.

"Hello?" I answered. No response. I was about to hang up.

"This is an automated call to inform you that your mortgage payment is past due."

Another reminder of how fragile the economy still was. I pressed zero to speak to someone.

"How can I help you?" the representative asked.

"I got a call about my mortgage being overdue in Florida."

"I'll need—"

"Yes, I know," I said, cutting her off. I gave her my name, address, Social Security number, and loan number.

"This loan is in default. I'll need to transfer you to another department."

I huffed in frustration. "Fine."

Another agent came on the line, and I had to repeat all my information.

"Hmm. Looks like your payment is three months behind," he said. "Before we continue, I need to inform you that this is an attempt to collect a debt. Any information obtained will be used for that purpose."

"I know," I said quietly. There it was again—**debt**. I bit my lip so hard I tasted blood.

"Are you calling to make a payment today?"

"No. My husband and I are divorced, and he refuses to make payments."

"Is your name on the mortgage?"

"Yes."

"Then you're responsible for the payments as well."

"You don't understand. He's supposed to pay the mortgage. It's in the divorce agreement."

"If you're having trouble with payments, we offer a modification program that might help."

"I tried. He wouldn't cooperate."

"I'm sorry to hear that. Without Michael's cooperation, the property will go into foreclosure."

"My house in Georgia is under contract, and I'll have the money by September."

"I'm afraid we can't wait that long. Payment is due now."

"Thank you," I said, and hung up.

I needed to get back to Florida and find someone who could actually help. Besides, my birthday was coming, and the last place I wanted to spend it was in Georgia.

Riley was asleep in his crate, strapped into the back seat. Unlike most cats, who yowl and panic in the car, he adapted to anything.

As I crossed the Fuller Warren Bridge into Jacksonville, I thought about how hard I'd worked for my independence. The Florida townhouse was my light at the end of that long, dark tunnel.

When I pulled up to the gated community, I punched in the entry code. The large wrought-iron gates swung open, welcoming me in like a pair of arms.

I'd promised myself not to get too attached to the place, but as I clicked the remote on my visor and watched the garage door creak open, it already felt like home. I drove in, and the garage door groaned down behind me. I sat in quiet darkness. Feeling my way to the kitchen, I flipped on the light. The peach-colored cabinets glowed under the overhead bulbs. The air was thick and stifling, but the new-house-smell still felt intoxicating. I turned on the A/C and stepped outside to open the main water valve.

I can't lose this house.

Chapter 46 | Short Sale

The Florida sun streamed through the window that morning. I smiled. Outside, half the townhomes on my block were still for sale, victims of the housing crash, but I tried not to think about that. After pouring a cup of coffee, I picked up the phone and called my mother.

"I'm here," I said cheerfully. "At the townhouse. It's beautiful."

"Are you going to sell it?" she asked.

"I don't know," I said, deflated. I'd fought so hard to keep one place of my own, and the thought of losing it to the same collapse that swallowed so many others made my stomach tighten. "I love Florida. I don't want to leave."

"Well, try to sell it before the bank forecloses," she advised. "You can always stay with me until you find something else."

"Thanks, Mom. I'll think about it. We'll talk later."

With a sigh, I poured another cup and walked across the street to the pool. It was always quiet—just me and the water. After a quick swim, I returned to the townhouse, sat at my desk, and sipped the last of my coffee as I searched online for a local real estate agent.

Maybe my mother was right. It couldn't hurt to try.

Listings were everywhere, discounted, desperate, foreclosed. Meritt Realty caught my eye. I jotted down the number and address — only five miles away — and tucked the note into my purse.

On the way there, I pulled to the side to glance at the canal, hoping to catch sight of the manatees. I reminded myself I couldn't keep stalling — the townhouse had to be listed.

As I stepped into the real estate office, a woman in a blue sundress greeted me warmly. Her nameplate read *Marci Ellis*.

"May I help you?"

"I'd like to talk to someone about listing my townhouse."

"Mr. Meritt is running a little late," she said with an apologetic smile. "You can make an appointment or wait if you prefer. He should be back soon."

"I'll wait," I said, choosing a cushioned chair in the corner.

Minutes later, a tall, handsome man in a sharp gray suit rushed through the door.

Our eyes met briefly before I looked away, and he walked past me into his office.

"Mr. Meritt will see you now," Marci said. "Third office on the right."

I walked down the hall and stopped in the open doorway. The same man from the lobby was now seated behind a desk. He stood and extended his hand.

"I'm Mark Meritt. Please, have a seat."

"I love the paintings," I said, looking around his office.

"My wife decorated the office," he said casually. "I'm not really a fan of Art Deco, but I haven't had time to change it."

"Oh," I said, trying to mask my disappointment. *Of course, he has a wife. All the good ones do.*

"What can I help you with?" he asked.

"I have a townhouse I need to sell. My ex-husband was supposed to handle the mortgage, but he stopped making the payments. I don't want it to go into foreclosure, so I figured a short sale might be better."

"It usually is," he said. "Since the crash, we've been doing more of them than regular sales. You'd still technically be in default, but the bank might forgive the rest of the debt. It'll take some time, and it's never easy." He paused, studying me for a moment. "We'll also need your ex-husband's consent."

"Okay," I said, though I had serious doubts Michael would cooperate.

"In the meantime, I'll run an analysis and find out the fair market price."

"Thank you, Mr. Meritt."

"Call me Mark," he said. "So… how do you like Florida?"

"I love it. I sold my house in Georgia. I was hoping to pay off the townhouse here, but I barely made any money."

He chuckled. "There are plenty of others. Let's get you out of this mess first, then we'll talk about finding you a new one."

On the drive home, thoughts of Michael nagged at me. I called again—no answer. So I called my mother instead.

"Florence! Why haven't you called today? I've been worried sick."

"Sorry, Mom. It's just been a long day. I found a realtor who's willing to list the townhouse, but he needs Michael's permission."

"Have you heard from him?"

"No. He won't talk to me."

"It's a shame he's so bitter, but I suppose he was hurt when you left."

"*He* was hurt?" I said, stunned. "Why does everyone feel sorry for him?"

I was finally able to contact Michael. Surprisingly, he agreed to sign the short-sale paperwork. It took weeks of back-and-forth with the bank. Michael showed up at my door the next week with a potted plant and a framed poem.

"I'm in town to sign the short sale agreement," he said. "Can I come in?"

I hesitated before stepping aside. "Sure."

"I'm sorry you have to sell this place," he said. "The mortgage payments were just too much."

I frowned. "If you'd helped me fix up the Georgia house like we planned, I could've afforded to take over the mortgage here."

He shrugged. "I heard you were seeing some construction guy from New York. Why didn't you ask him to fix it?"

I narrowed my eyes. "Who told you that?"

He waved it off. "Doesn't matter. He's not even a real contractor. Just a handyman."

"What's your point, Michael? Did you come here to help—or to stir up trouble?"

"I came because I thought maybe we could reconcile."

I stared at him. "It's too late for that."

"So you won't even try? Not even for a few months?"

"We *did* try. For thirty years."

"Forget it," he snapped, already halfway to the door.

"What about the papers?"

"Mail them to me!"

For a split second, I opened my mouth to say something—maybe explain, apologize—but he was already gone. I shut the door behind him and watched him walk to his car. Michael always had a way of making me question myself. I stood in silence, absorbing the heaviness of our broken past—the dreams we buried. But some doors are better left closed, and Michael's was one of them.

Mr. Meritt had been wrong. A short sale wrecked my credit just as badly as a foreclosure would have. My credit score tanked. Michael still wasn't speaking to me, but the alimony checks arrived each month like clockwork. At least that was something.

The townhouse sold quickly. I moved from room to room, trying to accept that I wouldn't be spending the second half of my life there. With my credit shot, there was no hope of getting another mortgage. I'd have to rent. I never thought I'd be back in an apartment. I decided to move in with my mother until I found a new place to live. The furniture would go into storage until I figured out my next move. I set shut-off dates for the utilities and spent one last night on the floor, wrapped in blankets. It felt like I was sleepwalking—sealing up the last box and watching the movers haul everything away.

The first rental complex I visited was close to my mother's neighborhood. It had all the bells and whistles—pool, tennis courts, a clubhouse—and even weekend barbecues with live music. Tempting, but it was cookie-cutter development: rows of identical units with steep rents. I'd lived in places like that before. I knew the novelty would wear off, so I passed on it.

I found myself pulled back to Vero Beach. I searched every corner of town until I spotted a small apartment complex. There was a park across the street. The location was perfect—right in the heart of the city, within walking distance to art galleries and restaurants. I called the number on the sign and left a message.

Then I remembered a listing I'd seen a few blocks away. I called and asked if I could see it. I drove over and waited in the parking lot for the owner to arrive.

The owner was kind and down-to-earth — no corporate management team to deal with, no endless rules. The unit was a two-bedroom. Sunlight poured in through five large windows in the huge living room. We walked down the hallway and peeked into the first bedroom. It was small — tight for my king-sized bed, but the second bedroom at the end of the hall was amazing. It had tall windows, just like the living room, and skylights lined the cathedral ceiling.

I stood there with my mouth open.

"It's facing the east so you can see the sun rise every morning."

I loved it! Without hesitation, I signed a lease.

There was no pool, but the beach was only two blocks away and over the bridge. Who needed a pool?

That first night, I was jolted awake by the deafening roar of a train. I hadn't realized the tracks were only two blocks away. It sounded like the conductor might lean in my window and shout, "All aboard!"

After a few days, I grew accustomed to it. The rhythm of that train — steady and unstoppable — reminded me that life kept moving forward. The sound, oddly enough, became comforting.

Then Daniel called. He'd decided to move in with me after all. Between the two of us, we'd be fine — more than fine. The fear of being alone began to fade.

Chapter 47 | A Stranger

The rumbling of an engine outside woke me. At first, I thought it was a train. It took me a moment to realize the sound wasn't coming from the railroad tracks. The roar of a motorcycle hurt my ears. It stopped outside my window. Compelled to check it out, I lifted the edge of the blind to peek through the slot. It was dark outside except for the streetlights. A man stood behind Daniel's truck. He wore a heavy black leather jacket, far too hot for summer. His face was hidden behind the shield of his helmet. Was he trying to hide his identity? Unlike other states, helmets were optional in Florida. He scribbled something on a small pad, then tucked it into his coat pocket and took off into the night. I went to the front room, overlooking the parking lot, and scanned the shadows, but saw nothing.

For the past few days, I had sensed someone was watching me. I slipped back into bed and curled up next to Daniel. Small, breathy puffs escaped him.

When he moved into the apartment, I thought my life would be more comfortable. *Will he ever get a job?*

When I met him, he was affectionate. Now, he doesn't kiss me and has no desire for intimacy. He said he was having erectile dysfunction issues. At first, I gave him the benefit of the doubt, but he never tried to see a doctor.

Our relationship evolved into something more akin to a friendship than a romantic bond. Comforted by being held in someone's arms, I turned a blind eye to reality. He was a warm body but nothing more.

The office wasn't far away, but I got caught up in the commute. Navigating the morning traffic, I darted between cars. Behind me, a black Impala did the same. It was hard to see the driver through the tinted glass. An uneasy feeling came over me. I sped up and cut in front of the car to my right. By the time I reached the office, the car had disappeared.

Silly goose! You're paranoid.

One month later, my alarm clock beeped, and I hit the snooze button twice. The third time, I knew I couldn't risk it again, or I'd be late for work. I carefully wriggled out from under Daniel's grip. His leg was draped over mine like a weight, his arm slung across my waist as if to say, *Don't go just yet.* I paused a moment, feeling the warmth of him beside me and the steady rhythm of his breathing. Forcing myself out of bed in the morning, I tried to look on the bright side. At least I wasn't alone. I took a shower, letting the warm water chase away my anxiety, then dressed and quietly slipped out of the apartment.

Crossing the parking lot, I noticed an old green pickup with Georgia plates—specifically, from Cobb County. That was where I'd lived before the divorce. What were the odds? I slowed down, staring at the rusted bumper and dented fender. Did I know the owner? Was it just a coincidence?

I shrugged it off and got in my car. By the time I was a few hours into work, I'd almost forgotten about it.

Then my phone rang. *Katherine,* the screen read. *My landlord.*

"Hi, Florence." Her voice was friendly, but something about her tone made my stomach tighten. "I don't want to alarm you, but yesterday a man came by asking about you."

"What?" I sat up straighter. "Who was he? What did he want?"

"I'm not sure. He didn't give his name. Just asked if I could let him into the building."

My pulse spiked. "You didn't let him in, did you?"

"Of course not! I told him I couldn't do that, and he left. But... I don't know, Florence. He gave me a bad feeling."

I pressed my fingers to my temple. "What did he look like?"

"Tall. Probably in his forties. Wearing sunglasses and a baseball cap. Said he was looking for a friend but wouldn't give any more details."

I forced a breath. "If he shows up again, please call me right away."

"I will. Don't worry," she said, trying to reassure me. "He can't get into the building without a key."

I couldn't shake the unease. I sat for a moment, staring at my phone, trying to make sense of it. Who would be looking for me now? And why not just call?

Maybe it was nothing. Maybe it *was* someone from the past—a nosy old neighbor, or an acquaintance from Georgia. I glanced out the window. The question lingered. *Who was he?*

Chapter 48 | Summons

The next morning, a message was on my desk at work, instructing me to call my landlord.

"Hi, Katherine. Is everything all right?"

"That man is back. He's trying to contact you on official business."

"What kind of business?"

"He wouldn't say, but he gave me his phone number and asked if I would have you call him."

I jotted down the phone number, tucked it into my purse, and went home. As I pulled into my parking space, there he was.

"Ms. St. John?"

"Yes. That's me."

He handed me a legal envelope. "What is this?"

"It's a summons for you to appear in court. I'm sorry about all the mystery, but I'm required to hand it to you personally." The man smiled and walked away, leaving me alone in the parking lot to read the contents of the envelope. The heading said, *Order on Plaintiff's Motion for Temporary Modification of Alimony.*

It was from Michael. He had agreed to pay me alimony until I was sixty-five, and now he was trying to stop it.

I ran up the stairs two at a time and entered my apartment. Daniel was sitting at his computer, scouring eBay for junk he could buy cheap and resell.

"Daniel. Remember that man who's been asking about me?"

"Yes." He said without looking up from his computer.

I waved the paperwork in frustration. "Well, I've just been served. Michael is taking me back to court to modify my alimony. According to this document, he's seeking judgment because I'm in a meretricious relationship."

"What does that mean?"

"According to this, 'A relationship is meretricious under the statute where a former spouse cohabits, and thus shares living expenses, with a party in a relationship that is similar or akin to marriage.'"

"That's stupid. We don't share expenses."

I frowned. Although true, it wasn't the time to argue about it.

"I don't recall anything in my final divorce papers that says I couldn't live with someone."

Searching through my important documents, I found my divorce papers and read them line by line. "No, there's nothing in here that says I can lose my support if I'm in a relationship. All it says is he has to pay me until I marry or turn sixty-five."

"So, you have nothing to worry about," Daniel said.

The court summons was not going to go away, so I called my lawyer.

"Mr. Davis is on the other line. Can you please hold?"

"Yes." I waited.

"Hello, Ms. St. John. I hope you're doing well."

"I was... until today. A man served me with a court order. Michael is trying to take away my alimony. He's claiming I'm in a what he calls, 'meretricious relationship.' I never even heard of that."

"Are you living with someone?"

"Well, yes, but we're not getting married or anything."

"How long has he been living with you?"

"I guess it's been two months now, but he still has a house in New York."

"Unfortunately, your ex-husband has found an old statute that defines cohabitation as dwelling together continuously and openly with another person, regardless of their sex."

"It's not true!" I wanted to tell him that Daniel didn't contribute to any of my living expenses. We didn't even have sex!

"You'll get a chance to dispute Michael's claim. Maybe I can get it dropped since you're no longer a Georgia resident. Fax a copy of the documents, and I'll get to work on them."

I hung up the phone and slumped into the kitchen chair, the summons still spread out on the table. My hands trembled. I wasn't sure why. Was it anger or fear, or both? After everything Michael had put me through, he was trying to take away the one thing keeping me afloat.

"What did the lawyer say?" Daniel asked.

"He's going to review the documents. He thinks he might be able to argue jurisdiction since I'm no longer living in Georgia. I don't think Michael lives there anymore either. That might be important."

Daniel grabbed a glass from the cabinet and filled it with milk. He went through a gallon a week. I shook it off. "So, what now?"

I didn't answer right away. Instead, I stared out the window at the parking lot, my eyes landing on the spot where I'd been served. The heat of embarrassment and helplessness rose in my chest. "Now I wait, I guess."

Daniel sat across from me. "You know this is just Michael being vindictive, right?"

"Maybe. But if the judge sides with him, I could lose everything. I can't afford this apartment without that money."

He reached across the table and took my hand. "We'll figure it out."

But would we? Daniel still didn't have a job. I was covering rent, groceries, utilities — everything. He kept promising things would be better once he was back on his feet. I had taken comfort in his presence, thinking two could live as cheaply as one, and at least I wasn't alone. Now, it felt more like a risk.

That night, I lay awake for hours, staring at the ceiling. A train thundered past at 4 pm, but even its familiar sound didn't soothe me. My mind raced. *What if the court sides with Michael? What if they decide that Daniel's living with me is enough to cut off my support?*

I got up and paced the apartment. The quiet was oppressive. Daniel was asleep, peaceful and unaware of the storm brewing around me.

I had fought so hard to rebuild my life. The apartment, modest as it was, represented safety, independence, and a chance to breathe again. I wasn't going to let it all slip away without a fight.

The next morning, I called Mr. Davis to confirm he'd received the fax. He had.

"We'll draft a response," he said. "And Florence — don't panic yet. These claims are hard to prove unless there's clear financial entanglement."

"But what about the part where they say it's like a marriage?"

"That's subjective. Judges don't love these kinds of cases. But we'll present your living arrangement honestly. It may come down to credibility and documentation."

"Okay. Thank you."

After we hung up, I took a long breath. My phone buzzed again — this time, a text from Michael.

"Nothing personal. Just time to reevaluate my finances."

Nothing personal? My blood boiled. After years of marriage, after everything I sacrificed, this is how he justifies pulling the rug out from under me?

Going back to court was going to be costly, but I wasn't about to go down without a fight.

Chapter 49 | Prying Eyes

A few days later, Mr. Davis called. "I'm sorry, Ms. St. John, but the judge refused to grant a dismissal on the basis that you're a Florida resident. I'm afraid you'll have to return to Georgia to answer your ex-husband's charges under oath and in writing. He's hired a private investigator."

"I had the feeling someone was watching me. Can Michael do this? Can he take away my alimony?"

"We'll fight it, of course, but let's take one step at a time. The first court date is one week from today."

"I'll have to take off from work and arrange a place to stay."

"I'm afraid so. By the way, is there any chance you can get your friend to move out?"

"If necessary," I said, but I couldn't bring myself to tell Daniel to leave.

After some digging, I discovered that Michael was indeed lying about his Georgia residency. The envelopes he sent with my alimony checks had listed Alabama as his return address. I made copies and sent them to my lawyer. If he could prove that Michael no longer resided in Georgia, the entire case would be thrown out before it even began.

I dressed and drove to see my daughter, Annmarie. We were going to lunch, something we hadn't done for a while. Michael thought he could divide us, and he did for a short period. In the end, he couldn't come between mother and daughter.

My granddaughter ran to me when I came through the door.

"Grandma, Grandma!" she shouted and hugged my legs. "I missed you."

"I missed you, too, baby."

My daughter had a strange expression on her face. She was staring at a cell phone.

"What's wrong?"

"Dad left his this at my house last week. I think you need to see what's on it."

She handed me the phone. The image was grotesque. A dummy hanging from a noose, dressed in a long, hideous gown with fake pearls. The caption read, "This is my ex-wife after I get done with her."

"What is this?"

"Dad had a friend watching you," she whispered. "I think he's living in your apartment complex."

A mix of anger and fear churned inside me. That rusty pickup with the Georgia tags flashed in my mind. It had seemed out of place, but I dismissed it, hoping, praying, that I was imagining things.

This wasn't just about alimony anymore. This was harassment. Michael had crossed a line. The man I married had once promised to love me forever, but was now plotting ways to he was to destroy me.

At home, I sat across from Daniel at the kitchen table and told him everything—the cell phone, the photo, and the stalker.

"Mr. Davis said it would help my case if you moved out before the hearing."

Daniel blinked. "You want me to leave?"

"No," I said softly. "I don't *want* you to. But I *need* you to. For now. Just until this blows over."

He ran a hand through his hair, then nodded slowly. "Okay. If that's what it takes," he said, but he didn't move. Not that night. Not the next.

And I didn't push him.

My lawyer sent me a list of questions called *Interrogatories*. Most of the inquiries were expected, like, "Do you have any joint checking accounts? Do you have debts together?"

Aside from my financial information, I was required to describe my educational background, including any degrees or certifications earned, and my criminal record for the past ten years, including all traffic offenses. They also wanted to know about my present employment and salary.

My fingers trembled as I read. What does this have to do with alimony? Alimony, I was entitled to for being married for thirty years.

The questions became increasingly intrusive as they continued. They requested a list of sexual relationships from the date of my divorce until the present. They even wanted a list of names for everyone who had stayed overnight at my home, and with whom I had ever spent the night.

Thank God my lawyer objected to this. He claimed the questions exceeded the permissible scope of discovery under the Georgia Civil Practice Act. The only purpose was to annoy, embarrass, oppress, and unduly burden me.

Daniel insisted on coming to Georgia with me. I feared the implications. In court, truth mattered, but perception mattered more. Still, I didn't want to face Michael alone, so I let him come.

Chapter 50 | Interrogation

The courtroom felt colder than I remembered. The judge's bench loomed ahead, austere and impassive, while polished wooden pews creaked under the shifting spectators. I sat at the defense table, heart pounding against my ribs like a war drum. I had come hoping the jurisdiction issue would end everything before it began.

The judge entered, his black robe billowing like storm clouds as he settled into his seat.

Mr. Davis rose, his voice clear, calm, and deliberate. "Your Honor, the plaintiff, Mr. Michael Corrigan, filed a motion to modify alimony, serving my client in Florida. However, jurisdiction requires that at least one of the parties have residency. Mr. Corrigan, we contend, is not a resident of Georgia but of Alabama. Therefore, we move for dismissal on the grounds of improper jurisdiction."

The judge didn't speak, but one brow lifted slightly. Mr. Davis seized the opening.

"If it pleases the Court, I'd like to call Mr. Corrigan to the stand."

Michael strutted to the witness chair as if he'd already won. His palm landed firmly on the Bible.

Davis held up the deed. "Mr. Corrigan," he began, "this document shows property you acquired in Alabama, correct?"

"Yes, but I live in Georgia. I have a warehouse."

Mr. Davis tilted his head. "A warehouse?"

"Yes, that's where I store my tools and exhibit inventory. I converted a trailer in the back into living quarters."

Mr. Davis turned to the judge. "No further questions."

Zimmer stood and launched into his counterattack with polished ease.

"Mr. Corrigan, have you considered yourself a permanent resident of Georgia since your divorce?"

"Yes," Michael snapped, triumphant. "That's where I register my vehicle."

"Objection," Davis cut in, but the damage was done.

"Overruled," the judge said, gesturing slightly. "Continue."

Zimmer's tone grew silkier, more self-assured. "So it was never your intent to establish permanent residency elsewhere?"

Michael gave him an arrogant smile. "No."

Zimmer looked pleased with himself. "No further questions, Your Honor."

The judge leaned back in his chair, steepling his fingers. A long silence followed. "Based on the evidence," he said finally, "Mr. Corrigan has maintained sufficient ties to Georgia. The motion to dismiss is denied. The case will proceed here in Georgia."

My stomach sank. Michael had twisted the truth just enough to slip through the legal cracks.

Then came the moment I'd been dreading. My last hope was to dismantle Michael's core claim—that Daniel Weaver and I were living together in a "meretricious relationship."

"Ms. St. John," the bailiff called.

My name hung in the air, and the courtroom transformed into a theater of humiliation. I walked to the stand on legs that didn't feel like mine. The Bible trembled in my hand as I swore to tell the truth.

Zimmer grinned like he'd been waiting to take me apart.

"Ms. St. John. Do you understand the penalties for perjury?"

"Yes," I replied, grasping to stay calm.

Zimmer's eyes narrowed. "Isn't it true that you are in a sexual relationship with Daniel Weaver?" The question sliced through me like a knife.

"No," I answered, voice level, though heat flared in my cheeks.

"But Mr. Weaver frequently stays at your apartment, doesn't he?"

"He visits," I said carefully. "He lives in New York."

"And yet his white van has been seen parked outside your apartment for days at a time."

I swallowed. "It's possible."

"Has Weaver contributed financially to your expenses?"

"No," I said again, the truth souring in my mouth.

"Is Mr. Weaver in the courthouse today?"

"Yes."

"Did you spend the night together at a hotel?"

"Yes."

Zimmer leaned back, triumphant. "Who paid for the room?"

"I did," I said, shame pressing against my chest.

"Objection!" Davis barked. "Relevance."

"Sustained," the judge said sternly. "Mr. Zimmer, move on."

Michael's attorney grilled me with a clinical precision that made my skin crawl. Nights with Daniel—the hotel room—his van parked outside my apartment. It wasn't just my finances on trial—but my dignity, my choices, my heart. I struggled to answer every question with restraint, forcing my voice to stay steady even as shame enveloped me. What bothered me most wasn't the accusations. It was how close some of them felt to the truth. Daniel had stayed over. His presence had brought me a strange mix of comfort and confusion. He had moved to Florida without promises or commitment.

Zimmer hesitated, his swagger briefly slipping. "No further questions."

The judge's gaze softened slightly as he turned to me. "You may step down, Ms. St. John."

The judge called for a recess. Only then could I breathe again.

Chapter 51 | Railroaded

As the courtroom settled into its rhythm, a hush fell over the room—a thick, unspoken tension blanked everything like an invisible fog. During the break, court staff rolled in a video screen and projector. A slow, creeping dread crawled up my spine.

What were they about to show? Could Daniel's emotional detachment somehow be twisted into proof against me? My pulse quickened. The thought of my life being dissected, frame by frame, in front of strangers filled me with silent panic.

When the judge returned to the bench, he slammed the gavel, and the next act began.

"Call your witness, Mr. Zimmer."

Zimmer smoothed the front of his jacket and straightened like a predator ready to strike.

"Your Honor, I'd like to call Mr. James Rosoto to the stand."

A short man strode forward with practiced assurance. After being sworn in, he spoke with the cool detachment of someone used to pulling secrets from the shadows.

"Please state your occupation for the court," Zimmer began.

"I'm a private investigator."

"And did you conduct any work related to this case?"

"Yes."

"Can you describe the nature of your investigation?"

"My objective was to determine whether Florence St. John and Daniel Weaver were living together."

A lump formed in my throat as Rosoto detailed his methods, including timing devices hidden under Daniel's vehicle, long nights of surveillance, photographs, and even video footage. The invasion of my privacy felt brutal, like being stripped naked in slow motion under the harsh courtroom lights.

When Zimmer tried to introduce the video as evidence.

Davis sprang to his feet. "Objection, Your Honor. This video was not submitted during the discovery process. It's inadmissible."

Zimmer raised his palms in a show of faux innocence. "I disclosed the investigator's name."

The judge wasn't impressed. "Disclosure of a name is not disclosure of evidence. What else can you present?"

Zimmer hesitated, jaw tightening. "If it please the court, I request to withdraw the video — for now." The blow he'd hoped to land never connected. Rosoto stepped down, his impact diminished.

Mr. Davis stood. "Your Honor, I'd like to recall Ms. St. John for redirect."

As I walked back to the stand, I felt every gaze tightening around me like a noose. The wooden chair felt colder, harder that time. Sweat pooled under my arms, betraying my effort to remain composed.

Davis's voice reached me like a rope in deep water—measured, calm, steadfast.

"Ms. St. John, do you hold the lease to your Vero Beach apartment alone?"

"Yes," I said, grateful for a question I could answer cleanly.

"Does Mr. Weaver keep personal belongings there?"

"No."

"Do you and Mr. Weaver share any joint bank accounts? Credit cards?"

"No."

"Has he ever contributed to your living expenses?"

"No. I pay my own bills."

With each answer, Davis unraveled the insinuations Zimmer had worked so hard to thread. He made it clear that there was no financial entanglement, no cohabitation, no shared life, just isolated moments strung together by assumption.

"No further questions, Your Honor."

Relief fluttered in my chest as I stepped down, but the next name sent it crashing again.

"I call Mr. Daniel Weaver to the stand," Davis said.

Daniel approached the stand. He raised his hand and swore to tell the truth, but it was his version of the truth I feared.

My palms grew damp.

Daniel sat on the witness stand, calm and collected.

Zimmer tried to twist Daniel's detachment, suggesting that he was freeloading and that I was supporting him.

Daniel stayed calm. Factual, even. "We're not in a monogamous relationship," he said plainly. "We're just friends."

The words hit harder than any cross-examination. I wanted him to be more than just a friend, even if I wouldn't admit it—not even to myself.

As Daniel stepped down, I stared at my hands. The court had seen what I didn't want to see. Daniel was not my partner, not in any way that counted. I had been defending myself in court while secretly wishing the defense wasn't true.

"No further questions, Your Honor."

The gavel fell, signaling the end of testimony. The judge ordered final briefs to be filed within thirty days.

With that, the court adjourned, but the battle was nowhere near finished.

Michael, determined to bleed me dry through legal attrition, rejected all settlement offers. This wasn't about fairness—it never was. It was a power play. He was dragging out the process, hoping to wear me down as my legal bills mounted.

That night, I wired Davis another payment. Money I could barely afford to spend. But what choice did I have? This war wasn't just legal. It was personal. And for me, survival meant more than just winning the case. It meant clinging to the last shards of dignity while the rest of my life fractured around me.

Without warning, Michael accepted the reduced settlement a week later. No explanation.

I never saw a refund from my lawyer, who claimed it had been absorbed by court costs—just another drain in a long list of losses.

Daniel needed to return to New York to check on his house, and I panicked.

"So you're abandoning me?"

"It's only for a month," he said casually. "You can come with me if you want."

Feeling raw and defeated, I called my mother.

"You should go back to Michael," she said without a hint of sympathy. "This Daniel doesn't love you."

"Neither does Michael," I snapped, but her words struck deep. Part of me feared she was right about Daniel. He was no better than Michael.

I didn't want to leave Florida, but the memory of crisp air, colorful leaves, and old familiarity up north was a temptation. I agreed to go, telling myself it was just a temporary arrangement. But Daniel had other plans.

Within the first week, he picked up a job at a local towing company. Before I could adjust, he announced, "If you help me, we can finish by spring and put the house up for sale."

"Stay here?" My voice rose. "All winter?"

The thought of braving a snowbound season in his drafty house made me shudder. I longed for the ocean, the sun, my apartment — my life.

I thought back to when I first met Daniel. Back then, after divorcing Michael, I had hope. Florida was a fresh start. I felt strong. Independent. Free.

Outside, the sun dipped behind the trees, shadows spilling across the ground. Why was I chasing a man who couldn't love me?

Daniel wasn't my future. He was a dead end. It was time to leave.

Chapter 52 | Life Coach

The journey back to Florida was quiet and cold. I stared out the window, watching the gray blur of the road, trying not to think. I had nothing — no savings, no partner, and almost no emotional reserves left.

When I turned the key in the lock of my apartment, a panic attack seized me. My chest tightened.

It was good to be back. There was so much I had to sort out, but at least I was back in Florida. Everything inside was exactly as I had left it. I unpacked my suitcase, went through my mail, which was mostly overdue bills, and berated myself for letting Daniel interfere with my alimony payments. Feeling sorry for myself and lamenting how drastically my life had changed, I felt ashamed — for leaving, and for staying. *Why did I always choose the wrong man?*

Desperate for clarity, I googled the question. That's when I found an article called "The Human Magnet Syndrome" by Dr. Ross Rosenberg. It explained how narcissistic people were attracted to codependent partners. The words on the screen hit like lightning. I was a magnet for broken men. I gave away pieces of myself like bandages, trying to patch wounds that weren't mine.

Daniel was a predator — he only played the part of being stable until he could hook someone. Someone like me. One fixer-upper after another. That was my pattern. Shattered men looking for help. And me — too eager to heal them, too blind to see the cost.

I reached for the dusty bottle of Sambuca we'd once saved for beach days. The thick, clear liquid burned as it went down, searing my throat. I continued reading.

What was wrong with me? Why did I keep settling for scraps, hoping they'd become something whole?

Maybe it wasn't about being needed. Maybe I didn't believe I deserved more.

Then I stumbled across a YouTube video titled "When You Grow Up Feeling Not Good Enough" by Lisa A. Romano.

I clicked play, and as her words filled the room, something inside me shifted.

My first *aha* moment. Codependency!

Growing up with an alcoholic father and an emotionally absent mother, I continuously tried to please them, but I never felt I was good enough.

Codependency shaped how I moved through the world. For the first time in a long while, the turmoil had a name. Codependency — not a weakness, not a moral failure, but a pattern. And patterns could be broken.

The truth had been there all along. It simply hadn't been visible. Walking in a fog—it was my coping mechanism. Without understanding the root cause, everything felt like floundering in the dark. Self-blame crept in—quiet judgments for not being 'normal' like other people.

I filled my mind with other people's thoughts, believing they might know better than I did.

Healing required understanding codependency. To do that, I needed help.

Could I correct my self-destructive behaviors? That question echoed in my mind. The truth was, I didn't know. But I was finally willing to try.

A group called Co-Dependents Anonymous (CoDA) met every week at a local church, and I decided to go. I began attending meetings regularly. Each time I walked through the church doors, I felt a little less like an outsider. Their faces became familiar. I began to recognize my own story in their voices, in their tears, and in the small, brave admissions they shared around the circle. There was a strange kind of comfort in knowing that I wasn't alone—that my pain and confusion were things others carried, as well.

I started noticing things, like how uncomfortable I felt when I wasn't fixing someone. How quickly I jumped to say "yes" whenever asked to do something for them.

I had built my entire life reacting to the needs of others, trying to avoid conflict, trying to be good enough to keep someone in my world.

What would it feel like to set a boundary and not apologize for it? To say "No," and mean it? To walk away from something that hurt, without carrying the shame?

That's when healing began—not all at once, not with fireworks—but in small, stubborn acts of self-respect. I wasn't broken. I was waking up.

Chapter 53 | Sailing

With the support of family and friends, I stayed on a path of healing. I still wanted to be in a relationship — but not yet. Dating at my age felt like sifting through garbage, hoping to find the least rusty can.

Everything was going well. Even Michael had softened, making small talk again. I knew he had motives, which made me uneasy, but I stayed civil — for the sake of our children and grandchildren.

When I visited my brother in Atlanta, Michael invited me out to dinner. I politely declined his dinner invitation. He even offered to continue paying alimony until my Social Security kicked in. I smiled, fully aware there would be strings attached. I had no intention of letting my boundaries slip.

That night, my brother and his wife took me to a local Mexican restaurant for dinner — live music, two-for-one margaritas, and a lively crowd.

By chance, one of my brother's close friends was there.

They greeted each other at the bar, and my brother waved him over to join us.

"Hi, I'm Gary," he said, pulling up a chair beside me. His arm brushed mine—at first, I thought it was accidental, but he made his presence known all during dinner.

Gary's southernly charm was disarming. And since he was my brother's friend, I let my guard down just a little. It felt good to be seen, flirted with, even if I wasn't sure I was ready for anything more.

By the end of the night, he had invited me to go sailing on his thirty-two-foot sloop.

I said yes without hesitation.

He zipped away in his Porsche. I couldn't help but smile. He seemed to have plenty of money. At least I knew he wouldn't be using me for his own gain.

When Gary arrived to pick me up to drive to the dock, his gray hair was windblown from driving with the top down.

I slipped into the passenger side and sank into the soft leather seat of his Porsche. He sped along the highway, the wind rushing past us. We didn't speak, but the silence wasn't awkward. I leaned back and thought, *I could get used to this.*

It was my first time sailing. The boat skipped across the lake, a fine mist spraying my face as we cut through the water. When it curved sharply at top speed, I gripped the edge and laughed, exhilarated. Gary stood at the helm, focused and confident. The outline of his muscles showed through his wet shirt— he looked good for his age.

Most men my age came with more baggage than Samsonite. But Gary had never been married and didn't have children. There was something refreshing about that—something uncomplicated.

"I'd like to see you again," he said, his voice gentle. "Maybe we can all get together before you head back to Florida." He gave me a soft kiss—warm, not demanding—and drove off.

That night, I went to bed thinking about Gary. I hadn't expected to meet anyone—not really—but something about him was different.

Florida was calling me home. I hadn't heard from Gary, so I chalked it up and drove back home.

Once I arrived, I changed into my bathing suit and drove to the beach. The sunlight danced across the rippling water like a thousand glittering coins tossed into the sea.

I closed my eyes as a gentle breeze tugged at my hair. The rhythmic crash of waves dulled the hum of my thoughts. I felt myself relax, as if the ocean had pulled my anxiety out with the tide.

My phone rang.

"I'm sorry," Gary said. "I got caught up with work and forgot you were leaving. I didn't get to say goodbye."

"That's okay," I said. "I'll see you next time I'm in Georgia."

"Ahh, I have to wait *that* long to see you again?"

We spoke on the phone every day, and the stranger in my life was beginning to feel a little less like a stranger.

Before long, he convinced me to drive back to Georgia and stay with him. Something tugged at my heart—that old familiar need to be wanted. My boundaries were slipping.

Chapter 54 | Saving Myself

Driving nine hours back to Georgia on a warm, sunny July day, I pulled into his driveway. His house was traditional, with a welcoming, lived-in feel. The scent of blooming gardenias lingered thick in the air. I breathed it in, walked up Gary's front steps, and rang the doorbell. No answer. I waited, rang again, then sat down on the top step and pulled out my phone to call him. It went straight to voicemail.

Now what? Do I sit here and wait? Leave a note and go to my brother's house?

Just as I was weighing my options, the door swung open.

"I'm so sorry," Gary said, a towel around his shoulders. "I was in the shower and didn't hear the bell." He stepped aside and waved me in. "Come on in."

He led me through a narrow hallway into the kitchen.

"You have a really nice house," I said, taking in the rustic woodwork and slightly outdated but cozy charm. "Did you design it yourself?"

"No, it came this way when I bought it. I'm not crazy about the wallpaper, but that stuff's a nightmare to take down."

I briefly considered offering my own wallpaper-removal tips — lessons learned from years of decorating disasters, but my codependency training kicked in. I smiled instead. "Yeah, I've had my share of wallpaper wars, too."

He opened the pantry and pulled out a few spices. "I hope you're hungry," he said, reaching for a large knife and chopping potatoes on a worn wooden cutting board.

"Can I help?"

"Nope. You just relax. I've got this under control." He smiled, tossing the potatoes into a glass casserole dish along with chopped chicken, onions, and a can of mushroom soup. He covered it with foil and slid it into the oven.

I'd always loved to cook, but lately, I'd been forgetting ingredients — sugar in my cookies, baking powder in my muffins.

"Voila!" he said, wiping his hands on a towel. "Dinner will be ready in about an hour."

"I can tell you know your way around a kitchen."

He shrugged. "I've been a bachelor forever."

"Oh, right. You never tied the knot. How'd you manage to escape?"

"Narrowly," he said, laughing.

After a very Southern dinner — crispy chicken, buttery potatoes, and sweet iced tea — we watched the sunset from his living room windows, which looked out over the western horizon. Two glasses of wine in, Gary moved closer on the couch and leaned in to kiss me. I froze.

"I'm sorry," he said quickly, backing off. "I didn't mean to come on too strong."

I wanted to kick myself. "Oh no—it's not that! I just haven't been with anyone in a long time."

We sank into the couch and watched sports until my eyes began to droop.

"Let's go to bed," he said gently.

Upstairs, I excused myself to brush my teeth and change while he pulled down the covers.

It felt strange—but also comforting. Gary didn't fill the silence with promises or pressure. He simply filled the space beside me. In a backward kind of way, we had started something. Most people date, ease into getting to know each other, and then fall into bed. We had reversed the order.

Wrapped in the warmth of his arms, I drifted into a deep and peaceful sleep.

In the morning, I quietly climbed out of bed and slipped downstairs to make coffee. Gary's cat waited for me at the bottom of the stairs, purring as I scratched behind her ears while checking my email. Gary slept in, and I didn't mind. I enjoyed the stillness of the early hour—the solitude uplifting.

"Let's go out on the boat today," Gary said when he finally came downstairs.

The thought of drifting on the lake again was exciting. Gary packed drinks and snacks—including wine. We jumped into his convertible and headed out under the glare of the Georgia sun.

Even though I had lived in Georgia for twenty-six years, it felt different. The air smelled fresh and clean as we sped along the winding roads, past trees that were green with new growth. On our way to his boat, country music blared from the speakers. There was no need for conversation, just a smile and an occasional touch.

Gary was an expert sailor, and I couldn't help but admire the way he worked the tiller.

"You try," he said, switching seats so I could take control.

Apprehensive, I grabbed the helm. It was disorienting at first, but I got the hang of it. The sails looked more complicated, and he took over. I stretched out at the back of the boat, content to let Gary and the wind do the work.

The heat was intense, but we cooled off by jumping into Diamond Lake. I wasn't a strong swimmer, so I hesitated at the edge.

Gary tossed a life preserver into the water. "Go for it. I've got you."

I took a deep breath and aimed for the ring, trusting that if I missed, he wouldn't let me drown. After our swim, we climbed back onto the boat. I stretched out on the deck, the warmth of the sun soaking into my skin, while Gary handled the sails.

"I love being out on the water," I said dreamily.

He tilted his head and smiled. "You could have this every day."

"Really? How do you figure that?"

"You could move in with me," he said.

"I need to go back to Florida. I have to work, you know."

"You could work here. I'll set up an office for you in one of the spare rooms. My house is yours," he added, his voice soft, sincere.

I laughed nervously.

"I don't want you to leave, Florence. I need you."

His words tugged at the deepest part of me.

"I love you," he whispered.

"I love you, too!"

Oh no... why did that just pop out of my mouth?

Gary seemed perfect. He was as sweet as the glaze on a Krispy Kreme donut — but part of me wondered what might be lurking beneath that sugary coating.

"Let me think about it," I said.

We slipped into bed, and I rested my head on his chest, listening to the steady thump of his heart. My mind drifted to places I didn't want to go. Deep down, I had known Gary wasn't a perfect fit. I turned onto my side and closed my eyes, putting my back to him and sinking into a restless sleep.

In my dreams, I watched myself in a scripted play, following Gary's lead, hitting my marks, reciting the lines.

Then a voice said, "When you continue to do the same thing, you always get the same results."

I woke in a cold sweat. The ceiling seemed to press down on me, the walls closing in. I couldn't breathe.

Gary wanted me to move back to Georgia, to a life I had already walked away from. For the first time, I stopped asking what would keep the peace or meet someone else's expectations.

I couldn't imagine giving up the surf, the salty breeze, the warm sand under my feet.

I had spent my life surrendering my choices to others. Not this time. This time, I decide.

The road to recovery is ongoing. But even when you take a detour, you can always find the way back.

Thank you for reading
Searching for the Shire
Please post a review on Amazon or contact
lamaisonpublishing@gmail.com

Other books by Florence St. John about codependency

Entangled
Queen of Hearts

Into the Sun

With a wounded heart
I traveled south
Into the warmth of your arms
Not knowing of the future
I succumbed to all your charms.

The moon hung heavy
In the clear sky
The sea raged to the shore
Reflections of afflictions
Emotions very raw.

I walked alone in silence,
Along the sandy floor
In quiet meditation
To a place within my core.

A path to letting go
Of things I had endured
Releasing tribulations
My future now secured

The morning sun shone bright,
And entered in my soul
A sense of true belonging
I knew that I was home.

Other Codependency books by Florence St. John

Entangled with a Sociopath
Queen of Hearts

La Maison Publishing
Vero Beach, Florida
The Hibiscus City